THE WEEKEND MAN

THE WEEKEND MAN

RICHARD B. WRIGHT

FARRAR, STRAUS & GIROUX

New York

To my mother and father

He knows death to the bone —

Man has created death.

W . B . Y E A T S

THE WEEKEND MAN

1.

Today there are three telephone messages on my desk when I return from my lunch-hour walk around the Shopping Plaza: three small yellow slips, rectangular in shape, and each entitled "Someone Called While You Were Out." When I began work here in September Sydney Calhoun, the sales manager, left several pads of these slips on my desk, along with a thick packet of memorandum paper, a *Webster's New Collegiate Dictionary*, a paperback *Roget's Thesaurus of Words and Phrases*, and a blue ball-point pen upon which are printed the words *Education Is Everybody's Business*. The Sales Department's secretary Mrs. Gerta Bruner has filled out the three slips and initialled them in her crisp capable way.

One message is from Sydney Calhoun. He called at 12:03, missing me by three minutes. He doubtless wanted to have lunch and talk over things. He does not want me to return his call.

Another message is from my wife Molly. She called at 12:24—at about the time I was ordering the Wednesday Special at the Woolworth's lunch counter in Union Place Shopping Plaza. Molly probably wants to know whether I have come to any decision about our future together. She would like me to call back later in the afternoon.

The other message is from Harold Pendle. Harold teaches English at Union Place Secondary School. He wants to write a grammar textbook and he phones me every three or four days to see if the project is still feasible, as he puts it. I always hasten to assure him that it is. According to Mrs. Bruner, Harold telephoned at 12:42 and he wants me to call him back. I will try to remember to do this before leaving the office.

These days I am earning my living as a salesman. I represent Winchester House, a small Canadian subsidiary of Fairfax Press of London and New York. You have probably heard of them, though you may not know that they have a Canadian subsidiary. We sell mostly textbooks, though we also have an excellent line of atlases, desk and classroom globes, map transparencies, language tapes, skill-testing question kits, overhead projectors, and Relex Count-Perfect Slide Rules.

I work out of a long low cement-block building on Britannia Road in Union Place, Ontario. Our building is new and has been painted a pleasing apple green. Inside, all is spotless and neat as a health clinic. As Fred Curry the office manager says in his monthly memorandum on the subject, we must all co-operate to ensure that Winchester House remains a pleasant place in which to perform our duties. This is sensible. My own office is a paradigm of tidiness and orderly work habits.

I am enjoying the work thus far and I like living in Union Place. Actually Union Place is a part of metropolitan Toronto; a large suburb which has wandered east of the city along the lakefront and then northward to meet the Macdonald–Cartier Freeway. It's much like the environs of any modern city: flat farmland which has been paved over and seeded with trim brick bungalows, small factories and office buildings, service stations and shopping plazas, all of it since 1950. In the last few years they've changed the zoning by-laws and now at least three or four dozen high-rise apartment buildings have climbed to the sky. Several more are now a-building and I spend many lunch hours watching the steelworkers crawl about on the girders of a new one at the corner of Mirablee and Napier Avenue. I myself live in one of these towering boxes; on the eighteenth floor of Union Terrace, only six blocks from Winchester House,

I am fortunate to live so close to my place of business; it's almost unheard of nowadays. It suggests an attractive orderliness to my life, but nothing could be further from the truth. As a matter of fact, my life these days is in a state of disorder and the phone calls from my wife will bear witness to this. There has been a great flurry of them lately, both at the apartment and here at the office (where I suspect Mrs. Bruner of listening in). Molly is really beside herself and it is difficult to blame her. She hates loose ends and it is a small miracle that she has put up with matters as long as she has.

On this grey December afternoon, a few days before Christmas, I sit and watch my fingers drum the surface of my chrome and plywood desk. I should be in the schools now. I should be talking to people about our new Tele-Visor Series 40 Projector. If you will buy one of these fine machines we will throw in a new and completely up-to-date atlas of East Africa. I have sold four Tele-Visors since September.

My colleagues are in the schools this afternoon. Even Sydney is making calls today. My window looks across to the parking lot at the side of the building and I watched Sydney step into his Oldsmobile not ten minutes ago. And yet here I sit, feeling rather vague and confused to tell the truth, thinking of Molly and my son Andrew and listening to Mrs. Bruner rattle the tea things outside my door. She will enter presently with refreshment.

On days like today when I am in the office Mrs. Bruner brings me a cup of tea and a biscuit at ten minutes to three. She places these victuals on my desk, frowning slightly, mindful of the fact that I am not out in the field with the other men. Mrs. Bruner hates a slacker. Out of the corner of my eye I watch her. She looks good today; blond and sleek and heavy-breasted in a starched blouse and a grey skirt which nicely covers her fine big bottom. Mrs. Bruner looks like James Mason's mistress in some movie about the fall of Berlin. I dare say she has climbed an Alp or two in her day wearing those heavy walking boots and short leather pants, singing songs of the Fatherland. Old newsreels from the Hitler years always have a few shots of little Hanses and Gertas climbing Austrian hills and singing hiking songs. Perhaps Mrs. Bruner appeared in one of them. As she leans across my desk I can see a vein throb in her long throat. Serving tea and cakes to the salesmen is the low point in Mrs. Bruner's day. She did not come to Canada to perform such duties. It offends her sense of the rightness of things. Mrs. Bruner attends evening classes at York University and

6.

when she has gathered enough credits for her arts degree she will unburden herself of all this in a memorandum to Sydney Calhoun. We salesmen will then pour our own tea.

The biscuits vary from week to week according to Mrs. Bruner's diet. She collects fifty cents from each of us and does the purchasing at the Bake-Rite store in the Shopping Plaza. I myself have watched her on lunch hours. She usually favours the digestive variety, though the current biscuit of the week is something called a cherry round, a fussy little affair of crunchy chocolate with a cherry filling. It must be in honour of the Christmas season. Three cheers for Christmas is what I say.

Mrs. Bruner's gelid grey eye has scanned my desk like the cold beam of a searchlight. It is useless to pretend that I am working when she is in my office. It does no good at all to shuffle papers and look busy, even though I'm clever at this sort of thing. I can keep few secrets from Mrs. Bruner. She knows when I am idle and there is nothing I can do about it. However, I am not really afraid that she will tell anyone. She will be content to punish me with her hostile silence. She will keep it all next to her heart.

I am sorry that Mrs. Bruner doesn't like me. This I find puzzling, for by all accounts I'm a likable fellow. Most people I meet take to me and, without saying as much, let it be known that I am A-Okay. Certainly I am calm and polite and an excellent listener. I make it a point never to give offence or disagree and since I seldom have an opinion on anything I easily avoid arguments, except with my wife. Most of the time I keep unto myself. I have no friends worth speaking of, nor do I seek any. I am the fellow boarding-house landladies remember as the nice young man who had the back room. I have had the back rooms of many boarding houses in my time.

Besides Mrs. Bruner there are only two other people I know who dislike me. One is a fellow salesman here at Winchester House and the other is my wife's mother.

My wife's father, on the other hand, is very fond of me and he would enjoy nothing better than to spend more time in my company. He thinks I am a queer fish and he would like to straighten me out. His name is Bert Sinclair and he is a public-relations officer with the Boulder Corporation. Bert is always giving me little talks and counselling me to find myself. He's convinced I'm lost. These talks usually take place on Saturday mornings at my apartment. We sit in the living room and have coffee and Bert leans forward in the basket chair and places a heavy speckled hand on my knee. Then he will say something like this: "Look, Wes. Every young man worth his salt has to search out those dark corners of his life. He has to explore any number of avenues before settling on his course. Some of the greatest names in our civilization have done just that. It's only natural and right. But there finally comes a time when a man has to stand up and say to himself, This is the road I'm going to travel. It takes courage but it's got to be done if a man wants to amount to anything." All this, of course, comes from one of Bert's old Shriner speeches. He was a Grand Sultan or something for years. But I don't mind, for Bert's a decent fellow and is interested in what I do with my life. Now and then he clips articles from the *Reader's Digest* and sends them along to me. I read one last night entitled "Let's Stop Knocking Faith." It was about a man named Clyde R. Wheeler who lives in Tulsa, Oklahoma. He's the sales director of a petroleum company out there. Mr. Wheeler shoots golf in the low nineties and performs the duties of elder in River Heights Presbyterian Church. What of it, you say? Plenty. Clyde R. Wheeler,

8.

you see, has no arms or legs and must make do with artificial limbs. It seems that he was involved in a bad car accident twenty years ago when he was just a travelling salesman like me. He was badly broken and burned and it took years to put him right with skin grafts and limb fittings. But he kept his faith throughout this ordeal and according to his wife Daisy even managed to remain cheerful, though how a man burnt to a cinder and without arms or legs can remain cheerful is lost on me. But it was interesting and I wish Clyde R. Wheeler well, though the story didn't leave me feeling as exalted as Bert probably would have liked. In fact, it left me quite hollow in the stomach. Of course I wouldn't dream of saying this to Bert. The next time we talk on the telephone or have coffee together I'll thank him for the article and tell him it made me think about the future. As a weekend man Bert will be glad to hear this. Weekend men are always pleased to learn that you are thinking about the future. What is a weekend man, you ask? A weekend man is a person who has abandoned the present in favour of the past or the future. He is really more interested in what happened to him twenty years ago or in what is going to happen to him next week than he is in what is happening to him today. If the truth were known, nothing much happens to most of us during the course of our daily passage. It has to be said. Unless we are test pilots or movie stars, most of us are likely to wake up tomorrow morning to the same ordinary flatness of our lives. This is not really such a bad thing. It is probably better than fighting off a sabre-tooth tiger at the entrance to the cave. But we weekend men never leave well enough alone. First off, we must cast about for a diversion. A diversion is anything that removes us from the ordinary present. Sometimes we divert ourselves into our own pasts. This is more likely to happen as we grow older. I am only thirty, for instance, but in the course of an average day I sometimes shake my head a dozen times to keep from sinking into my own past. Diverting oneself into the past would not be so bad if it didn't bring on the *nostalgies*. But, of course, it does, and a severe case of the *nostalgies* can often as not leave a person worse off than he was before.

It is also possible to divert oneself into the future; that is, look forward to something that is going to happen to you on Friday night or next July 23. This is all right except that it never happens the way you imagine it will: in fact, it's just as likely to turn into a disappointment. And that can plunge a person into the worst kind of despair. The weekend man simply never learns to live with the thundering ironies. He is forever looking backwards and being afflicted by a painful sense of loss or he is looking forward and being continually disappointed. What to do? Well, you'll have to work it out for yourself. I myself just drift along, hoping that the daily passage will deliver up a few painless diversions. Most of the time, however, I am quietly gritting my teeth and just holding on.

2.

I've been with Winchester House since the Tuesday after
Labour Day, school opening. Sydney says I'm coming along
fine, which means, I think, that he would like me to be a little more aggressive. He won't come right out and say so, however, because he heard at a sales seminar last month that
the days of the pushy high-pressure salesman are over. I've
been hearing this for years and I don't believe it. What I
believe is that the days of the pushy high-pressure salesman
are just beginning.

My work is not all that difficult and there is variety
enough to help me through the day. They loaned me an
automobile, a stiff little Dodge Dart, maroon in colour.

Now I have had the greatest enjoyment from this machine. I had never driven a car before, much less had one in my own parking slot, and though my Dart is only rented, it's mine now in spirit. I cherish its clean lines and six-cylinder engine and I give it the best treatment that money can buy, instructing the service people to use only those gasolines and lubricants recommended in the owner's manual. Still, I confess that the novelty of the Dart is beginning to wear thin and sometimes when I think too much about it I become quite gloomy.

As I said before, my work is not really difficult. It consists of travelling from school to school (I have eighty-two on my itinerary) and visiting teachers, usually heads of departments. My job is to persuade them to buy or recommend our books and equipment, though little actual persuading takes place. I usually just chat with them for a few moments in the teachers' lounges or in their offices—pleasant small talk. I try to be sympathetic to their problems. In the end I promise to send them a sample of whatever they're interested in, if it's not too expensive. Even then I sometimes send one along if the man seems interested. I never say very much about the books or equipment. I find the textbooks dull and heavy; even the anthologies of short stories and poetry are hard going for me and I could never convince people otherwise. Even if I did find a book interesting, I would never say as much. I've noticed that teachers don't want to listen to salesmen talk about *their* subject.

One night a few weeks after I began this job, I became interested in a senior biology text called *The Chain of Life*. It's a large handsome book with coated paper and hundreds of illustrations of plant and animal life. I was visiting a small Ontario town at the time and that night I sat in my motel room and read several chapters from *The Chain of Life*. The next morning when I called at the local high school I looked forward to talking to the head of the Biology Department. I found him in his classroom; a blond young man in a white lab coat. In his stiff smock which creaked and rustled when he moved, he reminded me of Richard Chamberlain, the young actor who used to play Dr. Kildare on TV. Fortunately he had a free period and he invited me to join him for coffee. He couldn't have been more cordial and we sat there in the empty classroom watching the autumn sunlight stream through the tall windows raising particles of dust in the air; drinking Nescafé from paper cups and talking about many things including the new hockey season and the chances of the Toronto Maple Leafs. But when I finally brought the conversation around to *The Chain of Life*, he became fidgety and began to rub a pair of tortoise-shell reading glasses with a soft cloth. I should have stopped, but I kept talking while he leaned back in his chair and lifted his feet to the desk. We were both relieved to hear the bell at the end of the period.

Afterwards, sitting in my Dart in the parking lot, I analysed the interview as best I could and I came to the conclusion that I had ruined an excellent relationship by going on about the book. It taught me a lesson. It's really more satisfying for everyone if I just send a copy of the book and let the person read it for himself. Once or twice Sydney has sent along a handwritten memorandum cautioning me not to be overgenerous, but the tone was very good-natured.

Our president, Harry Ingram, is in New York today. Harry is only a few years older than me; a brisk, likable man who fairly tingles with nervous energy. I like to watch him from my window in the mornings as he steps from his Buick Wildcat and walks across the parking lot. He has the springy step of a welterweight and I like the loose-wristed way he carries his worn brown attaché case.

Harry was sales manager at one of the older companies but he received a phone call from New York one Sunday afternoon. The next day he was on a plane for N.Y.C. and, to use Harry's words, "top level talks with the Fairfax brass." A week later he dramatically quit his job and formed Winchester House. He told me all this during my one and only visit to his office. Sydney had sent me in to be interviewed, but oddly enough Harry asked me very few questions, and talked instead of highlights in his own life. It was interesting and, as I've said before, I'm a good listener.

The staff at Winchester House is not large and most of them are girls who sit in front of business machines in the Accounting and Order Departments at the other end of the building. There is also a Shipping and Receiving Department down there and I often pass through this area on my way to the parking lot. The men who work down there seem to have a better time than the rest of us. They are nearly always laughing or playfully grabbing each other's genitals as they move among the tall stacks of books and atlases.

At our end of the building are the editorial, advertising, and sales departments. I don't know the editorial or advertising people well, though if I meet our chief editor, Cecil White, in the hall or washroom, I will pass the time of day with him. Cecil is a tall angular man in his late forties. He has a heavy sallow face and spaniel eyes. Cecil looks to be in the terminal stage of emphysema, but he still smokes several dozen American cigarettes each day. I can hear him now, hacking away in his office at the far end of the hall, dredging up a thick yellow-grey spittle which he deposits neatly into a Facelle tissue and drops into his wastebasket alongside crumpled packages of Camels. Cecil is a former high-school English teacher, a bachelor, an alcoholic, and a homosexual. He has several nubile girls working in his department. They are Honours English types with long hair and fine brows: extremely earnest in their manner. Cecil also employs a good-looking man named Tim. Tim has fine eyes and long yellow hair which always looks freshly washed. He's a very modish dresser and currently favours leather suits and buckled shoes. A lot of people around here make fun of him, but he's a self-assured young man and doesn't seem to mind.

The Advertising Department is run by a middle-aged spinster named Dorothy Lovitt. Dorothy still has a handsome figure, though it has thickened somewhat through the thighs and waist. Unfortunately, she has a long homely face with a prominent nose and mouth. And she must contend with the tiny black hairs of an incipient moustache which threatens to control her upper lip. In the early morning you can sometimes see the raw little razor burns. Dorothy is notoriously bad-tempered and has trouble keeping staff. Mrs. Bruner told me one day that Dorothy sees a psychiatrist each Friday, but I don't believe everything that Mrs. Bruner tells me.

There are only five of us in the Sales Department, though one of the more persistent rumours in our end of the building is that we will soon be getting another girl. Besides Sydney and myself, there are two other salesmen, Roger MacCarthy and Ron Tuttle, both excellent young fellows in their own ways. And, of course, there is Mrs. Gerta Bruner. She handles the correspondence and the phones.

For several minutes now I have been looking out my window across the parking lot to Britannia Road and the afternoon traffic. All day, heavy rain squalls have been coming in off Lake Ontario, pushing low dark clouds ahead of them. The merchants along Britannia Road switched on their neon signs almost an hour ago.

A dark blue Ford Galaxie with its lights and windshield wipers running rolls silently into the parking lot beside my little Dart. Roger MacCarthy climbs out and stands there with his broad back to me, locking his car door. He turns now and jogs through the rain towards our building, heavy-footed and bulky, like a tackle running interference, his coat slapping against his thighs in the wind.

Roger MacCarthy is a big jolly bachelor. He once played a lot of collegiate football and one of the professional clubs, Montreal I believe, was interested enough to invite him to training camp. But nothing came of it. Roger has a powerful body but he's neglected himself these last few years and he's drunk a great deal of beer. So he's turned soft and heavy and with his boyish face and brush cut he looks like a large friendly salesman when he smiles. When he is puzzled by something, he frowns and this darkens his brow and gives him a peculiarly menacing look. Before coming to Winchester House, Roger taught physical education in a suburban high school.

Roger has a problem with sex. He doesn't know how to go about getting laid and this worries him, as well it might, for he was twenty-eight last month. He has a tremendous interest in women, but he has trouble in making them understand this. I've noticed that pretty girls like Shirley Pendergast, who works in the Accounting Department, always thinks of Roger as a big good-natured older brother. They like him and they kid him all the time, but none of them would dream that old Roger is just dying to take off their pants and gaze at their little macaronis.

Shirley Pendergast comes around every fourth Friday

with our cheques. She's dark and slim, about nineteen, with the most exquisite ass you've ever seen, a perfect teardrop. Sometimes Roger is in my office when Shirley enters and she loves to watch his face grow scarlet. Shirley waves the cheque under Roger's nose and laughs with a tinkling sound. "Don't spend all of this on your girl friends, now, Roger," she says in her maple-sugar voice. And Roger, all wound up like a mainspring, will finally draw out something like, "Oh yeh, and who's that fellow I see picking *you* up every night in the red rag top." Shirley smiles slyly at this, pleased as the dickens. "Just *you* never mind about that, eh!" she scolds. Then she walks out, flicking her neat little ass towards our dry throats and leaving a faint scent of My Sin lingering in the fetid air of my cubicle. Oh my!

That fellow in the red convertible they're always talking about is a tough-looking young man with long greasy hair and dirty fingernails. He spends his days pumping gas at the Shell station on the other side of the Shopping Plaza and he probably spends his nights grabbing and squeezing that beautiful ass. Roger jokes about him, but I think he must hate his guts and would enjoy working him over a little bit in some dark alley.

When Roger is in town he likes to come into my office and talk about hockey or football or girls, mostly girls. He wanders in around nine o'clock dressed in baggy grey slacks and a Harris tweed jacket with leather elbow-patches. He usually paces back and forth, glancing out my window from time to time, jingling the change in his wide pants or fingering the porcelain ball paper-weight on my desk. He considers me a man of the world because I'm married but now live separated from my wife. This gives me a slightly raffish air in his eyes.

3.

At four o'clock Molly calls again. "Wes? Where the hell have you been? You were supposed to call me back."

"I'm sorry, Molly. One or two things came up."

Molly's voice is as brittle as the ice that forms on puddles these wintry mornings. I can see her, sitting before the telephone desk in the dark hallway of her father's fine old home. At this time of the day she's probably just returned from visiting Andrew at the Fortescue School and is now on her way downtown to shop for Christmas. No doubt she's wearing a smart tweedy suit and her long brown hair will be piled neatly under a simple hat. She's probably drawing on leather gloves at this moment and looking a bit like Joanne Woodward in one of those scenes where

Joanne is trying to get rid of some creep so she can rush off to meet Paul Newman on the steps of the Natural History Museum.

"Wes? What have you been up to these last few days? I've been trying to reach you at the apartment. There's never any answer there."

"I'm out of town a lot these days, Molly. I'm a travelling salesman now, you know."

"Uh, huh. Listen. I'd like you to have dinner with me on Friday night."

I can hear Roger MacCarthy laughing outside my door. He is telling Mrs. Bruner about an amusing little incident that happened to him in the schools today. Roger is one of those persons who is always living through some amusing little incident. If he were a mortician and the city were struck tomorrow by a calamity, Roger would still find an amusing little incident in the day's events and tell you about it when his work was finished. Molly is speaking to me in her cool throaty way.

"Wes? Are you still there? Will you have dinner with me on Friday night at Martino's?"

"Yes. Yes, of course, Molly. What time?"

"It doesn't matter. Eight o'clock?"

"Eight is fine."

A splendid silence while Molly works those gloves into place, stretching the excellent leather over her long fingers, her head tilted to one side, with the telephone resting easily in the cradle of her shoulder. She must look great.

"Wes? You will be there, won't you? You won't pull any nonsense this time?"

"No nonsense, Molly."

"I mean to talk business, you know. I want this thing cleared up. I can't go on like this."

There is a pause that stretches further than either of us

1 9.

would really like. Her words sound more and more theatrical in the silence, dangling helplessly in the air like lines from an old Bette Davis movie.

"All right. Let's say Martino's at eight on Friday."

"Right, Molly. I'll see you then."

She hangs up quickly and my heart sinks. Damn and double damn. Why can't we at least be civil to one another? Again my fingers commence their little tattoo on the desk. My throat feels parched. I will tread softly to the fountain in the hall.

Gliding past Mrs. Bruner's desk with my smile firmly in place, I approach the water fountain. Typewriters are hammering around me. Rosemary is bent over the fountain, her long jet hair falling across her face. Rosemary is one of Cecil White's girls—dark and serious with melancholy eyes and a nice trim body which she doesn't look after. She has a pasty complexion and it wouldn't surprise me if she suffers from constipation. She needs more sun and more green vegetables.

"Hello, Rosemary."

She lifts her fine head and gives her hair a little toss. A tiny blue vein throbs at the base of her temple.

"Hi," she says, smiling, and hurries away to her office down the hall.

At one time I thought Rosemary and I might enjoy a small romance. Sometimes these quiet brainy ones surprise you by jumping into the sack at a moment's notice. And sometimes they do the strangest, most delightful things. During my first weeks here I chatted with Rosemary nearly every day, leaning against the doorjamb of her little office during morning coffee break. One Wednesday I took her to lunch at the Woolworth counter in the Shopping Plaza and we talked passionately about poetry and John Keats.

Rosemary is devoted to poetry and Mr. Keats. She told me that she did a paper on him in her final year at Victoria College and I expressed an interest in seeing it. We both left the lunch counter in a state of intense excitement. I was all set to invite her to my apartment when overnight a chill developed between us. The temperature dropped alarmingly and the great solemn river that flowed between our souls congealed to ice. Rosemary was mine no longer. I suppose she learned I was married, though I never bothered to ask. Anyway, it finished our poetry talks and now whenever we meet in the hall or at the fountain she bolts like a frightened hare. I don't mind really, for I wasn't that interested. It was only a little diversion I thought we both might enjoy.

Rosemary now has a boy friend who meets her several times a week at the front of the building. He's a tall pale youth with shoulder-length blond hair and steel-frame spectacles. I would guess he is a graduate student bent on a teaching career. I often watch them walking hand in hand across the parking lot to his sensible little Volvo; Rosemary in flat shoes and wide pleated skirt, the graduate student in beige jeans, light army surplus jacket and desert boots. They suit each other.

Rosemary is having a good time now, dreaming of their life together. She is dreaming of rainy autumn evenings when they will sit before the fireplace and watch the flames dance against the walls. And listen to the wind high in the trees. He will read poetry to her.

"For God's sakes, hold your tongue and let me love," he will read, standing tall and lean by the fire. Afterwards they will make love on the rug and it will be a hymn to Beauty. Ah, Rosemary—you will read poetry all right, but silently to yourself. The graduate student will mark term papers in the next room, sitting erect in his chair. You will lie abed together and perform the act of love with immense seriousness and purpose. But Mr. Keats will murmur in your heart through it all and you will be in the garden with him and his sad grey face and his nightingale. One day you will abandon the whole thing and dream anew of the time when your two pale children grow up. Then you will teach people about Mr. Keats in the winters and you will spend your summers in Italy and Greece, searching for something among the ruins of heroic civilizations.

As I step towards my office, I can see Ron Tuttle making his way along the hall, shaking the rain from his hat and swinging his briefcase. He stops at each doorway to smile and greet people, like a man running for public office. I hurry to avoid him. He will not stop at my office door, for I keep it closed, and anyway Ron doesn't like me.

Ron Tuttle is in his middle twenties; a small neat man with thinning blond hair. He's a very natty dresser. He's also the hardest-working man I've ever met. When he's not telephoning teachers or making appointments with the secretaries at the Board of Education, he is writing reports or memoranda on recent sales trips. Sometimes these memos are marked confidential and sent direct to Harry Ingram in sealed interoffice envelopes. One day some weeks ago I walked into Ron's office when he was drafting one of these special reports and he slipped it under his desk blotter while we talked. This sort of thing drives Sydney crazy, but there's not much he can do about it. Ron is Harry Ingram's favourite. He hired him away from another company and likes to think of Ron as a bright young protégé.

Sydney respects Ron's ability and diligence, but he doesn't really like him. He thinks that Ron is after his job, and he's right about this. Ron believes Sydney is a jerk and a muddler and there's some truth in that too.

Aside from his considerable duties here at Winchester House (he's our best man and has the toughest territory), Ron is taking a course three nights a week in data-processing. He is several jumps ahead of the rest of us, as he explained to me one windy day in the parking lot shortly after I came here.

"Wes," he said, striking a smart blow against the hood of my Dart with a gloved hand. "Listen here. What happens if tomorrow we wake up and find out that Fairfax Press has been sold to one of the big communications systems, RCA maybe or IBM. This happens every day. These people are *interested* in publishing. Now where does that leave Winchester House?"

He paused and flipped up the collar of his topcoat, waiting for me to say something. I had no thoughts on the subject.

"Well, suddenly we've got a new set of bosses, right?"

"Right," I agreed, looking past Ron to a tall girl from the Advertising Department, one of Dorothy Lovitt's latest finds. She was fighting a stiff breeze as she climbed into her Triumph. Suddenly a gust of wind lifted her billowing skirt and revealed a deep thigh and garter belt.

"And maybe they don't like the way we do things up here," Ron continued. "Where does that leave us, eh!"

"I'm not so sure, Ron," I replied, watching the girl coolly tuck those legs beneath the dash of her tight little car.

"It could leave us right out on our ear, that's where," Ron said, growing excited at the thought of us all out on our ears.

"But listen, Wes," he said, "they look twice when they learn you've taken the trouble to find out about these latest techniques in business accounting. Hell, everybody in business today should know a little something about computers."

2 3.

I nodded, smiling, and watched the Triumph sputter into life. It left the parking lot trailing a thick blue exhaust. I remember thinking that if only I knew something about the internal-combustion engine I could approach the girl and offer to change her oil. We both watched the little car slip into the traffic stream on Britannia Road, and then Ron turned to me again.

"You should look into all this, Wes," he said. "It's a very exciting thing."

I agreed with him, of course.

4.

The tall girl in the Triumph is no longer with us. She had a craggy face but the most exciting long legs. I am thinking about those legs now. And Rosemary. Rosemary's legs aren't at all bad either. If only she didn't cover them in those dark stockings and dumpy skirts. I am thinking of Rosemary and the tall girl. Both of them are naked and they are in bed with me. I am naked too. The bed is round and huge like a giant hassock. We are going to have an orgy on this hassock, the tall girl, Rosemary, and I. I am lying on my back waiting for the fun to begin. The tall girl is blowing softly on my feet and Rosemary has wiggled her tongue into my ear. She has bad breath, but that's all right. There is an erection under my desk.

They say strenuous exercise relieves these longings. Perhaps a brisk jog along Britannia Road through the darkening afternoon. The truth is that I am now living through a famine. In this day of liberated womanhood and sensible contraception it is ridiculous to be sexually deprived, but there it is. I have been living through this famine for over four months. My glands barely function these days. In the bathroom this morning I examined my organ, poor pitiful shrunken thing that it is. As a matter of interest, it was with my own sweet Molly that I last lay down in love.

One humid Friday towards the middle of August I sat in my apartment watching Matt Dillon's peaceful horse-face as he stepped into a tense saloon and cooled things out. It was an old episode of *Gunsmoke* and Chester was still limping around and talking in that outlandish way. I have no air-conditioning and the apartment was stifling. It faces west and catches the full blast of the afternoon sun. From time to time I would get up and walk to my balcony, which overlooks the Shopping Plaza and several other grey apartment buildings. From there I would peer through my German-built telescope, which I had carefully mounted on an aluminum tripod for stability.

I bought this telescope several years ago when I had a brief flirtation with that old and respectable branch of science called astronomy. This was just before I met Molly, and she was greatly excited to learn that I often arose in the cool morning hours to gaze at the heavens. It helped to confirm her belief that I was destined for great things. I mostly use this fine hand-crafted instrument now to watch the summer girls on the roof of the next apartment building. It's not as tall as Union Terrace and it has a little sundeck on the roof. In the summer the girls like to lie up there on Saturday mornings with their bottles of Quik Tan and their paperback copies of *The Carpetbaggers* and *Valley of the Dolls*. Oh, I'd like to get my hands on one or two of them when they are in the middle of those spicy books!

I also enjoy looking down at the Shopping Plaza, particularly on Thursday and Friday nights when the young suburban families arrive in their sleek cars to load up at this fabulous market place. I like to watch this innocent custom of our land. Like a Sunday-morning bird-watcher, I am now able to recognize several families and can chart their course from the Mister Do-Nut Shop at one end of the Plaza to the big A & P at the other end.

Sometimes when I tire of looking at the shoppers in the Plaza, I turn my telescope a few degrees to the northwest and watch the traffic moving along the Parkway. And on this particular Friday night I was doing just that, watching the city empty as the cars streamed northward to the lakes and cottages—an endless and unbroken line of gleaming metal. The drivers were just flicking on their parking lights as the big orange sky deepened and softened into dusk. And rising above the haze of the lower city like a strange dark bird was the Tom Thumb Traffic Helicopter beating its way through the soupy air.

I stood watching the helicopter when my telephone rang. It was my father-in-law Bert Sinclair and he sounded his usual cheerful self.

"Wes? How the devil are you?" he asked.

"Is that you, Bert? I'm fine, thanks."

"How are things going, son?"

"Not too bad," I said.

Bert cleared his throat.

"Look, Wes . . . how about coming over to the house? It's going to be a corker tonight. You'll suffocate in that darn apartment."

This was true. There *was* a hot rumpled look to the place. The sink was filled with dirty Melmac and a film of dust lay over everything. In the background I could hear Bert's television: little explosions of canned laughter. He wasn't watching *Gunsmoke*, for at that moment Matt was drilling two cowboys on the main street of Dodge. I watched him as he walked over to where they lay, that hang-dog expression on his face. Oh shoot, why must there be all this senseless violence in my town. Then I spoke.

"Well, this is good of you, Bert, but I don't think I should, really."

"It's all right," Bert said, laughing. "Molly and her mother are up at the cottage. I guess I'm what you call a summer bachelor, ha, ha."

"Ha, ha. Well." This was tempting. That dark old house with its cool oaks and elms.

"Come on over, son, and have a cold drink with me now."

"Bert," I said, wanting very much to tell him what a decent human he really was, "I'm going to take you up on that. I'll be there in an hour or so."

"Good lad. Bye, bye."

"Bye, bye, Bert."

Old Bert likes me. Of that there can be little doubt. As I mentioned before, his wife Mildred does not share his opinion of me, but Bert has always been loyal and kind. Even when I perched on the arm of the Sinclairs' sofa, holding Molly's damp hand, and informed them that their daughter was pregnant by me, Bert merely shook his big head and made a clucking sound with his tongue. Mildred raised long fingers to the temples and rolled her eyes. I waited tensely for the cerebral haemorrhage.

"How could you? How could you?" she muttered, sinking into a chair. Bert fussed around her, fetching pillows and patting them into place.

"Now, Mother," he said quietly, "it's all right. Everything's going to be all right."

"Oh, Bertram, be quiet and bring me a glass of water," Mildred said finally, frowning at all of us.

Afterwards Molly and her mother talked in an upstairs bedroom while Bert and I sat in the kitchen listening to the hum of the electric wall clock. We each drank off a large glass of Scotch and Bert reached over and squeezed my knee with thick fingers. His heavy face was pale and blotchy.

"You'll be all right, son," he said in a sickly voice. "Everything's going to be all right."

Then he took our glasses and rinsed them under the tap, drying them carefully with a yellow dishtowel.

The Sinclairs live on Brattle Street in Rosedale, a rich and leafy enclave in the centre of Toronto. I can make it from Union Terrace in about an hour, taking two buses and the subway. That Friday night in August, Bert greeted me at the door, a large florid man in khaki shorts and canvas shoes. With his moon face and Joe E. Brown mouth, Bert looks like a comic from some Hollywood musical of the early forties, one of those birds who was always taking pratfalls while his good-looking straight man buddy was getting the girl. I saw one of these old movies the other night on *The Late Show*. It starred Don Ameche, Linda Darnell, and Jack Oakie. Bert's a dead ringer for Jack Oakie.

"Come on in, son, for heaven's sakes," Bert cried, steering me through the doorway. He was grinning widely, a little tight.

The house was cool and dim. For some reason Bert had most of the lights out except for the kitchen, where a luminous blue glow played along the control panel of the electric stove. Bert mixed the drinks by this unearthly light, splashing Bacardi rum over the ice. He looked across at me and shook his great head, making a kind of snorting sound deep in his throat.

"Wes, when the hell are you going to stop this foolishness and settle down into a sensible job?"

"I don't know, Bert," I said. "One of these days, I guess."

Apparently Bert had invited me over for another talk about my future. Now he crunched an ice cube between his teeth and rolled the broken pieces from jaw to jaw. There was a long pause during which I could hear the burr of the refrigerator motor and, from an open window, the sound of a dance band playing an old song called "The Carioca." At that moment I experienced the most fantastic *déjà vu* of my life. Somewhere in that kitchen, floating around in the warm dark air, was a half-forgotten fragment from my past, so close and so elusive. Bert took another swallow of rum and looked over at me again.

"I hear this night-watchman stuff is finished," he said.

The question tugged me forward. The fragment floated past and out the window into the night, gone forever. I blinked.

"Yes, I quit a couple of weeks back. I enjoyed it, though."

I had been working as a night watchman in a storage elevator on the Toronto waterfront since early spring. It wasn't bad work. I had the shift from midnight to eight. The idea of walking home to bed in the morning has always had a great appeal for me. I also like having my weekends in the middle of the week now and then. Tuesdays and Wednesdays were my days off.

I spent most of the time napping in a tiny office or listening to an old Marconi mantel radio owned by the man who had the shift before me. The reception was very good and I could easily pick up the chatter of disc jockeys in places like Hartford, Connecticut, or Raleigh, North Carolina. I had to get up three times a night and walk through the buildings. I couldn't believe that anyone in the city of Toronto would go to the trouble of stealing a sack of oats or barley; still, I had to make these so-called patrols thrice nightly. My only companions were the pigeons who roosted high on the steel rafters and sometimes shat on me as I walked beneath them. From time to time, just to keep them on their toes, I would slam one of the heavy iron doors and listen to the panic as the dusty air filled with the whirring sound of their wings. After a few moments, though, they would settle down and I would direct the beam of my five-cell EveReady along the girders. And there they would be, hundreds of them, fat and grey, making that peculiar warbling sound.

By the middle of summer, though, I grew tired of the heavy dank smell of the waterfront and the breezy disc jockeys and the pigeon shit. Of course, I didn't tell any of this to Bert. I'm sure he was not really interested in why I left. He considered the job bizarre and was just pleased that I was no longer a night watchman. Now he slowly massaged his scalp with the fingers of one hand and addressed a question to the clock.

"So what's next, Wes? Where do you go from here?"

"To tell you the truth, Bert," I said, "I'm not sure. I suppose I could go back to Mr. Kito for a few weeks. The fall is always a busy time for him."

Mr. Kito is a landscape gardener. I've worked on and off with him for three or four years. Bert sighed and leaned against the sink counter. Like many big men with barrel-shaped upper bodies, Bert has absurd legs. They are utterly hairless and no bigger around than a turkey's. As he shifted his weight against the counter, two thoughts struck me. One was that the sort of conversation we were having, the sort of conversation we always have when we meet, might be appropriate, even sensible, if I were two years out of university and still trying to find myself, as Bert puts it. The other thought was that gents like Bert should never wear short pants.

"Mr. Kito," he finally muttered. "Darn it, Wes, that's not what I mean." He waved his glass towards the bottle. "Help yourself there."

I poured another drink while Bert rolled his glass between his palms and softly chuckled.

"What a character you are! I've never seen the beat of you, boy."

Bert always says something like this when we talk. After nearly five years I still manage to astonish him. For all I know, he is right. Perhaps he never has seen the beat of me. He sighed again and sank slowly into a chair.

"I'm going to tell you something, though," he said, tapping the table with the bottom of his glass. "I still believe you and Molly can hit it off together." He cleared his throat and suddenly looked grave as a verger. "That girl of mine is still very much in love with you. But I'm going to tell you something and I want you to listen, because I know Molly. Indeed, I think I know her better than anyone, perhaps even better than you."

This statement was both false and true, as statements like this often are. Molly's nature is too complex for Bert and he doesn't really know his daughter very well at all. But it is possible that he knows her better than I do, for there are times when I confess I don't know her at all. She's a total stranger with a familiar face. At other times I think I know her too well. Bert poured himself another drink.

"I love you two kids, you know that. I want to see you work this thing out together. There's nothing I want to see more." He swallowed the drink and shook his head again. "You know you're both two peas in a darn pod when it comes right down to it. Both of you too independent to get along."

He paused. A tremendous wave of gas was rushing up his throat. He tucked his chin back against his collarbone to fight it off.

"Now listen. I still believe that the two of you can work this thing out together if you'll only give and take a little. I know Molly's a little demanding and maybe over the years we've indulged her a little bit but you're far from blameless either, Wes . . . Now you know what I think?"

"What's that, Bert?"

"I think you're both smart as whips, and don't think for a minute I'm flattering you, young man."

Bert was now about to affect his air of good-natured gruffness, the better to scold me gently for my aimless ways.

"Now, Wes. Molly may still love you and I believe she does. But I know as well as I know my own hat that she isn't going to settle for the wife of any landscape gardener or night watchman. She's an educated woman, Wes, and it's just not in her. She's not built for that kind of life. Now she deserves a decent measure of security and support. No one's asking you to be the president of the Royal Bank but you've got to look to your responsibilities. All right, you pay your share, Molly has told me, but there's more to this than money. Now I think you've got a great future once you square yourself away and apply yourself. But time's a-wasting, Wes. And none of us are getting any younger. You're thirty years old and you should be squaring yourself away. Now Molly's been undergoing quite a bit of strain lately. These last few weeks have been hard on her. With the boy and everything . . . it's not easy to go it by yourself . . ."

Bert always refers to his grandson as the boy. Andrew is a Mongoloid child.

". . . you should know that by now."

"I know it."

"Well . . . what are you going to do about it, son?"

"I don't know."

"Do you love my daughter?"

"Yes."

He smacked the table so hard I jumped.

"There you have it. Really now this is so silly it isn't funny. Here are two bright attractive young people who openly admit they love each other and still they can't manage to work this thing out. . . . You know you should both be ashamed of yourselves and I've told Molly as much, so don't think I'm picking on just you . . . listen . . ." He leaned across the table. "Will you do your father-in-law a favour?"

"Sure thing, Bert."

"Will you talk to somebody who's looking for a good man right at this moment?"

"What does he want this good man to do?"

Bert leaned back in his chair. "I've always thought you could sell, Wes. Now don't misunderstand. I'm not talking about the door-to-door or used-car stuff. I'm talking about professional salesmanship of a high calibre. I believed it when you were with us at Boulder and I still believe it."

"Thanks," I said, "but I'm not so sure about that. I haven't sold anything since *Liberty* magazines twenty years ago."

"Well now just you listen. A chap I know named Syd Calhoun has bought the cottage next to mine. You know the Parkinson place. It's been up for sale since the old man died a year ago. Syd bought it in May and he's put a lot of money into it. Looks real nice."

"Yes?"

"So Syd's sales manager of a publishing company. It's a small company and fairly new but they're in a terrific field. It's a field I wouldn't mind getting into myself if I were thirty years younger. Education is just going boom these days, you know." He flung both hands into the air to illustrate the boom.

"Syd's looking for a man right now and I took the liberty of mentioning your name. When I told him you were a college man and had once been with us he sounded interested. It looks like a great opportunity to me. There's a tremendous future in education." He paused and finished his drink. "So what do you think?"

"About what?"

"About this job with Syd. Will you go and see him? Talk over the prospects. See if it suits you?"

"Sure, Bert. I'll be glad to."

He reached over and patted my arm. "Good lad."

Now with the air cleared and the promise of my future renewed, Bert relaxed. We both settled back and began to enjoy one another's company, like two businessmen who have completed a deal. Bert made some chicken sandwiches and we ate these with cold beer, sitting on folding chairs on the flagstone patio at the rear of the house. It was a fine evening, moonless and fragrant with the smell of freshly watered lawns and damp flower beds. A breeze came by to stir the warm air and dry our brows. Things were looking up. Bert wheeled out a portable television and we watched an old movie called *Young Man with a Horn*. Kirk Douglas plays the part of a young man who wants to be the world's best jazz trumpeter. He manages to accomplish this, though he almost ruins his life and the lives of those close and dear to him. It works out well in the end, however, and he marries Doris Day, who was always there by his side during the lean times.

Bert was feeling flatulent during the movie and every so often his big stomach would let out a deep growl. Each time this happened he would look over at me and grin shyly.

"It's those darn ribs I had for supper, Wes. They always repeat on me."

The movie didn't interest him at all and after a while he dozed off. Now and then he broke spicy wind and this awakened him and he mumbled apologies. I didn't mind. Farts don't bother me. I fart a lot myself.

I slept in Bert's bedroom that night, dressed in a pair of his pyjamas which I secured at the waist with a safety pin. Before retiring I stood in front of the dresser mirror and tried on Bert's Shriner's fez—an elaborate headpiece royal purple in colour with a silver tassel and a gold crescent moon and three small stars on the front. It came down over my eyes and made me look like some sly rascal from the streets of old Baghdad.

Some time in the night I awoke with a premonition. Somebody was in the room. Sure enough, there was Molly of all people standing at the foot of the bed staring down at me. We both started at the sight of each other.

"What in God's name are you doing here?" she whispered fiercely.

"A guest of your father's," I whispered back. "I thought you were up at the cottage with your mother."

She sat down on the edge of the bed and lighted a cigarette. In the flare of the lighter she looked haggard, her fine eyes dark with worry. She was having a bad time.

3 6.

"I felt like a drive. I ended up here." She shrugged her shoulders. My poor Molly! For as long as I've known her, she's suffered from these numbing bouts of insomnia. The only cure for it is to climb into the MG and streak down the black roads with the throttle open and her hands placed lightly on the stiff steering wheel. I was always amazed and delighted at the way she handled her little car, even when the speeding tickets came in from village constables all over the province. Molly always returned after these dark journeys to ask for love and fall exhausted into sleep. This strange visit now stirred memories.

"Are you sad, Molly?"

There was no answer as she stared hard at the glowing end of her cigarette. From down the hallway I could hear the drone of Bert's giant adenoids at work. I reached out and touched her arm.

"Come and lie down beside me, Molly."

"I'm going to bed, Wes . . . in my room."

"We are man and wife."

"Oh, very clever."

"Don't be so blue. Things aren't that bad surely."

"Shit."

"Come and lie down now."

I drew her down beside me and she lay there stiff as a plank.

"Molly, I miss you. Do you know that? I want you to come back and live with me."

The silence thickened between us. Somewhere in the trees outside the window a night bird called to his mate. I placed a hand upon her wondrous thigh. Oh, those great legs, firm and strong from how many games of field hockey at St. Helen's! What number of badminton matches or volley-ball leaps produced that gentle swell of calf or rising thigh?

Oh, St. Helen's I cherish you and your sensible athletic programme! Thanks be to the games which strengthen and preserve the vitamin-enriched bodies of these great thumping Rosedale girls. As for myself, I never pass by your handsome gates and watch the new crop in their dark jumpers and oxfords without remembering moments like this and murmuring my thanks to the headmistress and the board of governors.

I placed a hand on Molly's stomach and watched her crush the cigarette into an ashtray on the night table. She gave a heave and exhaled a lungful of smoke, throwing an arm across her forehead. I gave her leg a gentle squeeze.

"You'd like to fuck me, wouldn't you, Wes? That would make everything right, wouldn't it?"

"Not everything," I said.

"I am so damn tired of all this."

I felt a nerve twitch along her leg. She sounded so stricken that I took her hand. She quickly pulled it away.

"Things are going to damn well change . . ."

". . . yes . . . they are."

She sat up suddenly and hugged her knees to her chest. "Christ, Wes . . . when are you going to start acting like a man? We can't go on like this." She shook her head violently. "Good God, I'm twenty-five years old . . . everything is rushing by . . . I want more than this . . ."

". . . now Molly."

"No, I really mean it, Wes . . . there has to be more than this . . . oh, what am I going to do . . . God . . ." She began to rock back and forth hugging her knees, moaning softly to herself. "Goddamit I want Andrew home with me. But I can't care for him here. Can't you see that? This place is hopeless. Mother doesn't want him. I just know it . . . she's ashamed of him . . ."

". . . easy now . . ."

"Oh, Wes, it's true, damn it. She is ashamed of him . . . and Daddy . . . he's just bewildered by it all. And what about you?" She turned towards me, her eyes glistening like pools. "Living in your own weird little world."

Now she laid her head on her knees and cried. I sat up and put my arms around her—another sorry scene in the lives of Mr. and Mrs. Wes Wakeham. And is anything but the poet's fancy ever in harmony with these anguished moments? It's doubtful. Through Molly's low terrible sobs came the sound of her father's ludicrous buzz-saw from down the hall—wheezing and whining in a veritable comedy of noise. And so we clung to each other on Bert's bed, like shipwrecked survivors on a raft.

"All right now, Molly," I said after a moment. "I'm going to see a man about a new job next week. He's a friend of your father's. We'll see how things go."

"I know you love him, Wes," she cried softly. "You visit him every week. The nurses have told me."

"Of course I love him . . . for Christ's sakes . . ."

The sobs were dying slowly and I could feel her fingers in the flesh of my arms. She dabbed at the corner of her eyes with a Kleenex.

"Damn it, Wes, I know we could make it if we only tried a little harder."

Molly's system has inherited her father's quick recuperative powers. Now she was recovering her old tough grip on things.

"It's so easy to bugger everything up, isn't it?"

"Easy as pie."

"I don't want it to happen to me."

"I don't think it will," I said, kissing her cheek.

"Do you love me?"

3 9.

"Yes."

"I really think you do, you know . . . in your own odd way." She touched the side of my face tenderly. "What job are you going to see about next week?"

"Salesman in a publishing house."

"Publishing?" She sounded pleased.

"Yes."

She absently worked a hand under Bert's pyjamas and began to stroke my chest. She was already building dreams—mixing a six o'clock whisky and soda for her tweedy pipe-smoking publisher husband while he explained some intricate move in the boardroom.

"Who's Daddy's friend?"

"A man named Calhoun."

"Oh Lord," she laughed bitterly. "Syd Calhoun. Oh, you'll love him, Wes. He's a prize. You really will."

I squeezed her thigh like a schoolboy.

"If only you'd try, darling," she whispered, "just try for once. I know you could do anything you really set your mind to."

"Great Scott, Molly. I'll eat them to pieces, just you wait."

"Oh you are a prick," she said good-naturedly as she sank a long tooth into my shoulder.

O the sweet joy of the unexpected! The blessed bliss of being in the right place at the right time! Plan a thousand seductions if you will. Spend hours, days, weeks on stratagems. Trim your candle and uncork your wine; fill your incense-burner and fiddle with the knobs on your stereo. Only give me now and then a piece of arse that comes hurtling out of the blue, for no piece is sweeter to my taste.

During the second week of our marriage Molly bought a book on the delights of coitus. All her St. Helen's chums were reading it to their husbands and girl friends. Molly used to talk about it on the telephone with her friend Ernestine Hough. It was filled with pornographic etchings and the wicked thoughts of some priapic Oriental who dwelt among us a thousand years ago. *Now gently take thy beloved's firm member and annoint it with the fragrant balm.*

When I came home from the Boulder Building, Molly would be sitting on the bed, cross-legged and naked with the sun streaming in and this book on her lap—open to a gilded drawing of dancing goats and lovers entwined on a grassy hill. There was fruit in a bowl and a bottle of wine on the night table. In those days we lifted the telephone receiver early and locked the doors at sunset. Thumbing through those ancient recipes for pleasure, we copulated like the beasts of the fields. *Now mount thy beloved with care, stroking her precious parts the while.* The book was a bestseller and translated into thirty languages. Our copy now gathers dust in a closet next to Molly's tennis shoes. All those variations on a theme, but after much monkeying around Molly is partial to sitting on it. I don't mind. Any way is fine with me so long as the organ isn't permanently damaged or even badly bent.

O my lovely wild and well-bred Molly! Astride my poor hips like some pagan queen on her slave, uttering terrible oaths and thrusting her long narrow breasts into my mouth.

Later I watched her sleep through the first light. The room was filling with shadows, and manic birds were tuning up the pale sky. By the window the dark leaves brushed against the house like dry whispers. Bert had descended into silence at last, after one final cataclysmic snuffling which must have rolled him onto his stomach. The house was filled with sublime peace. I should have been grateful for the moment. Instead, I could only lie there wishing that all this had happened to me on a Monday or a Wednesday.

5.

The snow is wet and heavy, falling through the yellow light onto the parking lot. The traffic along Britannia Road moves fitfully with a dark hissing sound. Winchester House is almost deserted. Mrs. Bruner just looked in on me with her direct grey eyes.

"Going to burn the midnight oil, Mr. Wakeham?" she asked, buttoning up her car coat. My staying in the office all day has really upset Mrs. Bruner. I have let the side down and this has annoyed her. She will probably complain about me to Mr. Bruner tonight over the boiled potatoes and ham. They will discuss my future in German while their two teen-aged children talk about teachers and basketball.

From my window I watch her cross the parking lot to her Volkswagen; a blond good-looking woman with firm calves and a steely grip on life. She and her husband Helmut landed in Canada twelve years ago with two small children. Now her husband earns good money repairing television sets, and when Mrs. Bruner finishes with the evening classes at York University, she will be worth another couple of thousand a year. They own a three-bedroom home in Union Place and have two Volkswagens. Mrs. Bruner told me the other day that Helmut is thinking now of buying a small used Mercedes in the spring. They are thrifty and confident citizens of this new land. Mrs. Bruner's only worry is that we will let too many black people into the country. It's a favourite subject with her.

A few typewriters are still clacking away in the Editorial Department as I wrap myself in my new Suburban All-Weather and switch off the light. The door to Ron Tuttle's office is open. During the day when he is writing his confidential reports Ron keeps his door closed. Along towards five o'clock, however, when most of us are getting ready to call it a day, Ron likes to open his door and sit there, looking at the papers on his desk with a frown. As I pass by his door tonight I wave and smile.

"Night there, Ron."

Ron looks up showing me his teeth, which are small and white and perfect.

"Say, Wes, how's it going?"

"Splendid. Couldn't be better."

Ron leans back in his chair, locking his hands behind his head.

"Were you out today?" he asks smiling.

He has already asked Mrs. Bruner this and he knows the answer. He is acting more and more like a sales manager.

"Not today." I am grinning fiendishly. "A day of paper-work."

"Well, there's always lots of that, isn't there?"

"Too much, Ron, too much."

"Ha, ha, ha. You can say that again, boy."

We are both laughing like lunatics. Ron dislikes me intensely. I can feel it coming across his desk in small cold waves.

"Well, good-night now, Ron."

"Night, Wes. Looks rough out there tonight," he calls after me. "Hope you got your snow tires on."

"Right. You bet," I shout back, stepping through the building at a brisk pace. Ron will also gravely consider my future tonight, sitting in the dinette with his thin mousy wife, Marion. She, however, will want to talk about the two boys and how they are slowly driving her insane.

The wind breaks forth in gusts from the lake. It has grown much colder in the last few hours. The large damp snowflakes are quickly churned to slush along the glistening streets with their cheerful service centres and office buildings lighted now by the cleaning people. Behind these busy avenues the open crescents of Union Place are filling with snow and Christmas lights are winking from the windows.

I don't think I would drive to work every day if I had any say in the matter. I would enjoy walking now and then, but my line of work demands an automobile and so I carefully manoeuvre the Dart onto Britannia Road and turn southward. I am still not entirely confident behind the wheel and this is my first little taste of winter driving. Mercifully I am always going against the traffic, which is now locked bumper to bumper coming north. Over the radio Tom Thumb can scarcely contain his glee.

"This doesn't look like a very jolly night, Mr. Motorist,"

Tom says in his squeaky voice. "Things are looking very, very weird all over. We have tie-ups and rear-enders on all the major arteries leading out of town. You might say that tonight the old town is suffering from hardening of the arteries. Ho, ho, ha, ha. Anyway, this little baby is going to drop seven or eight inches on you people tonight, so it looks like a late supper for everybody."

At the corner of Britannia Road and Union Avenue I stop for a red light before making my turn. On my right the Shopping Plaza is afire with colour and light—an enchanting fairyland in the snow, as the Union Place Chamber of Commerce Development brochure describes it. On the roof of the Arcade Department Store a giant Santa Claus in a rocket ship blazes into neon brilliance every few seconds with the words: Countdown to Christmas—Only Three More Big Shopping Days Till Zero Hour. I've spent several lunch hours watching the workmen erect this sign and each time I pass it I try grimly not to think of that grey day next month when they will return to dismantle it. Through the car windows I can hear a song from the Plaza loudspeakers. A brassy orchestra is playing and a chorus is singing and humming a song called "Winter Wonderland." I can catch a few of the words. These words are, "Sleigh bells ring. Are you listenin'? In the lane, snow is glistenin'."

On my left in the northbound lane is a big dark Chrysler. It has just made it across the intersection and is crouched now, next to me. The driver is in his early forties—a heavy-set man with a flaring regimental moustache. He has the sheepskin collar of his coat pulled up around his ears and on his head rests a nifty green Alpine fedora. The little hat looks strange on the big head, too friendly and open for the fierce military face. The Moustache and I find ourselves staring out at each other and, as so often happens in situations like this, we both look away briefly and then return again at the precise same moment to stare into each other's eyes once more. Our heads are in perfect synchronization. It is embarrassing. One can look away and fiddle with the radio dial or check the fuel gauge, but there is an irresistible urge to look back. And so we watch each other, though his look is turning into a glare. He probably thinks I am a homosexual. He doubtless would like to get out of his Chrysler, pull open my door, and smash me right in the mouth. Perhaps even give me a kick in the scrotum as I lie on the pavement. I cannot tell the Moustache that all I am doing is searching his face for something to go on—some clue that will help me understand how he does all this without blowing his brains out some Monday morning about ten minutes past seven. Now I do honestly believe that he would like to step from his car and place a meaty hand on my throat. But the light turns green and I press the accelerator, negotiating my turn safely, as the driver's instruction booklet recommends.

There is a large plastic tree in the lobby of Union Terrace and there is Christmas music in the elevators on this snowy evening. Perry Como is singing "O Little Town of Bethlehem" accompanied by a choir of at least five hundred boys and girls. In this cubicle crowded with fur coats and parkas we rise solemnly to our floors staring at the lighted numerals above the door. One or two are humming along with Perry and the kids. At the eighteenth floor I step from the elevator clutching three envelopes plucked from my letter box.

In my apartment I sit in the basket chair and read my evening mail. The first envelope contains the notice of a Fantastic Year-End Inventory Clearance Sale at Sam Fine's Clothing—*Fine's for the Finest*. On December 24, the card announces, prices on all top-quality suitings will be *drasti-*

cally slashed to make way for new stock. Bring this card and take advantage of a *truely unique offer.*

In the second envelope is a piece of cream-coloured cardboard. In green and red ink are the words: *Dear Tenant: Season's Greetings and Best Wishes for a Prosperous New Year. Yours truly, Union Property Management and Development Corp.*

The third envelope contains a Christmas card from Harold Pendle. And goddamn! Didn't I forget to return Harold's call today? The card is a colour snapshot of the Pendle family: Harold and his wife, a tall, plain woman with a large face, and their two long-haired leggy daughters, each about ten years old. They are all seated on a sofa in what must be Harold's living room. They are all smiling with their hands folded neatly in their laps. On the back of the snap are the words *Merry Christmas to All of You from All of Us, The Pendles.* I must phone Harold tomorrow.

My evenings usually begin with *The Early Show*, which I watch while preparing and eating my dinner, though sometimes, for variety's sake, I will switch off the TV and eat my meal looking at the blank screen. I do this even when there is a movie I particularly want to see. On Monday night they showed *Casablanca* with Humphrey Bogart and Ingrid Bergman, a priceless old jewel which I have seen a dozen times. There is a famous scene in that movie where Bogart walks into a bar smoking a cigarette. The piano player is playing a song called "As Time Goes By." This song gives Bogart a bad case of the *nostalgies* and he tells the piano player to knock it off. It's good stuff and I would dearly love to have seen it again, but I had been watching *The Early Show* for a couple of weeks and it was time to break the pattern.

I watch a lot of television, mostly movies, though my

favourite show is called *Run for Your Life*. This is a weekly series about a rich good-looking young man who has this terminal disease. An actor named Ben Gazzara plays the part. The doctors have given him only a year to live. He travels around the world and spends a lot of time standing on the balconies of expensive hotels, staring into the night, while beautiful women fall in love with him and weep when they discover they can't have him. Every moment of Ben's life is sharpened and heightened by this awareness of his own doom. He has no future at all—only the great quivering now. Actually he's the luckiest man alive and he's having the time of his life. In fact, if I had any say in the matter, that's what I'd call the programme, *The Time of His Life*.

Television is a good diversion. There are people who pull long faces and groan when they hear talk like this. They prefer to pass their time by reading books or learning bridge or studying anthropology. I used to read books and in my day I've subscribed to a few rough-papered quarterlies too. I even sought out people who were interested in talking about such things as the role of the individual in a techno-logical society. Listen—I once paid several hundred dollars for a German telescope to study the stars and another time I sent for a brochure on a short-story writing course. None of these things is as good as television.

This evening there was a science-fiction movie from the early fifties called *Them*. It set off a little tingle of nostalgia. I remember taking a girl named Mary Lou Gassner to see it years ago at the Odeon in Middlesburgh. The movie frightened her and she sat very close and squeezed my hand all night. Later we stood in some shadows by her house and exchanged hot open-mouthed kisses for half an hour. I remember it was a clear winter night with a silver moon in the sky and we stamped our feet in the snow to keep them warm. After the kisses we worked our hands inside each other's coats and we talked about this movie and the end of the world and the possibility of life somewhere on the hibernal stars above us.

Them is set in the New Mexico desert near several A-bomb testing sites. All these tests have produced a great deal of radiation and with curious results. It seems that something especially odd has happened to the ants in this desert. All this radiation has triggered some genetic malfunction and they grow to be eight feet wide. Naturally they pose a threat to mankind and the story centres on the attempts of a gentle old entomologist played by Edmund Gwenn to eradicate these giant ants. It's quite an absorbing film and I watched most of it leaning on the counter of my kitchenette, wondering what Mary Lou Gassner was doing at that exact moment, and waiting for my Shake 'n' Bake fish dinner to cook.

6.

My brother Frank phoned tonight. He phones every year about this time to invite me to spend Christmas with him and Kitty and the children. They especially like to see me when they learn that Molly and I are not seeing each other. They don't like Molly. It's never been said in as many words, but I know they think she's too high-handed and indifferent.

Before we were married Molly used to drive me up to Middlesburgh on Sunday mornings in her little open car. We would knife across the flat Ontario countryside, along black roads past the red brick farmhouses and the unpainted barns with their aluminum roofs gleaming in the sun and the Holstein cattle standing under the trees. Before the railway crossings and the village signs Molly would gear down smoothly, pushing the stubby floor lever ahead with a gloved hand. The little car would shudder and whine to the slower revolutions of the engine, sometimes giving off a deep thrumming sound and exploding into backfires which raised sparrows from the roadside bushes. On we would coast through some village where the late morning heat lay along the road and the solitary white church was surrounded by the farmers' Plymouths. Once we stopped the car near a church to watch a crow flap his heavy wings across the treetops and listen to the voices singing:

Jesus calls us! O'er the tumult
Of our life's wild restless sea!

We always arrived at Frank's in time for lunch, looking cool and windblown and jubilant, like the young people you see in the automobile advertisements.

Frank and Kitty were always glad to see us, but I could tell they didn't approve of Molly or the red MG or anything about her style. Molly was pleasant towards them, but distant. Frank and Kitty bored her with their small-town chattiness and she was always glad when I would suggest that it was time to leave.

After our marriage we visited them a few times and Molly made an effort to get to know them. But there was nothing there for either side and she finally gave up. After that we saw them only once or twice a year, even though Middlesburgh is only a hundred miles from Toronto.

These telephone calls from Frank have a ritual all their own. Frank is seven years older than me and we've never been close. When he telephones he always manages to sound gruff and protective, summoning forth that tone of mock severity used by all older brothers when talking to younger brothers they've never really known. I usually come in for a scolding, so that instead of asking me to spend Christmas with them, Frank might begin this ceremonious call by actually *telling* me to get my ass up there for the holidays.

"What have you been doing with yourself, for Chrissakes?" Frank asks angrily. "We haven't heard from you for weeks."

They never hear from me for weeks.

"I've been pretty busy, Frank, the new job and everything."

"Yeh. How's it going?"

"Fine. It's working out well."

"Good . . . look . . . you're coming up here for Christmas, right? . . . And no shit now. . ."

I can hear Kitty laughing, hushing up Frank about his language. Frank is having a few tonight.

"Well, I don't know yet, Frank, I'll have to see."

"See hell. You get up here . . . Look, you're welcome here any time, you understand that?"

"Sure, I understand that."

"Okay . . . now listen carefully . . . if you don't spend Christmas with Molly and her people, I want you up here with us, all right?"

"All right, yes."

I begin to laugh. If I were up there in the living room, Frank would punch me hard in the bicep and tell me I don't eat enough.

"We'll see, Frank. I'll let you know."

"All right, but take it easy, eh! Here's Kitty."

Kitty's soft girlish voice is full of affection. "Hello, honey. What have you been doing with yourself? We haven't heard from you for ages."

"I've been busy, Kit, the new job and everything."

"Uh, huh. I hope you're enjoying it."

"Yes, it's fine."

Kitty takes a deep breath before proceeding. She's always in trouble when I mention my current job. She used to ask me all sorts of polite meaningless questions about my work. It was her way of being friendly. I wouldn't see them for months and then one Saturday night, overcome by some mysterious longing, I would catch the nine o'clock bus for Middlesburgh. I would sit in the last seat of the half-empty coach, reading a paperback detective novel and sipping rye whisky from a pint bottle between my legs. How I loved those lonely journeys! At the bus terminal I would phone them and they'd come for me. In the car Kitty would ask these questions about my work and I'd have to tell her that I was now doing something altogether different. She'd laugh and call me a terrible gadfly, but I could tell she felt foolish about the whole thing. Now when I mention my latest job she just takes this deep breath and leaps across the entire subject. I'm just as glad.

"Are you going to spend the holidays with us, Wes?"

"I don't know yet, Kit. I can't say for sure. If you could give me a couple of days."

"Sure, honey, but you know we'd love to have you."

"Yes, I know."

"It's real Christmassy up here now. We had quite a snowfall last night. The children love it. Everything looks so clean and white."

"I'll bet it's lovely."

I feel a sharp pang for those white streets of my childhood and the snow falling in perfect silence through the yellow light from corner lampposts.

"We're trimming the tree tonight, Wes, and having a drink. As I guess you've already gathered." She laughs.

"Good. Well, have one for me, eh!"

"Look . . . the kids want to say hello to their uncle now."

"Fine."

"Remember now . . . you're welcome any time."

"Thanks, Kitty."

This too is part of the ritual—the children's Christmas greetings to their uncle. I don't mind really. They're good kids. I can hear Kitty's careful whispered instructions, including the reminder to ask about Cousin Andrew. Twelve-year-old Donny is first, his thin choirboy's voice piping through the wires.

"Hello, Uncle Wes."

"Hi, Donny. How are things?"

"Fine thanks. How is Andrew?"

"He's very well. And looking forward to Christmas just like you. . . . Are you playing hockey this year?"

"Yes sir. Every Saturday morning at the Arena."

"Good, I wish you luck."

"Thank you. Merry Christmas and I hope we see you."

"Right. The same to you, Donny."

Sharon comes next, nine years old, fair, and lively like her mother.

"Are you coming up for Christmas, Uncle Wes?"

"I don't know yet, sweetheart, maybe."

"I sure hope so and I hope Andrew can come too."

"Well, I don't think that'll be possible, but we'll see. Okay?"

"Okay. Bye."

Now I hear Kitty lift three-year-old Bonnie to the receiver, whispering to her, "All right now, darling. Sing your song for Uncle Wes like a good girl. Mommy'll hold the phone."

I listen for the tiny voice but Bonnie is suddenly and mightily overwhelmed by a fit of shyness and seems reluctant to perform. It used to be Donny singing "Rudolph the Red-Nosed Reindeer." Then Sharon came along with the "Chipmunk's Christmas Song." Finally Bonnie breaks forth excitedly into a breathless sing-song version of something called "Santa Claus Has Landed in His Whirly-Bird." It demands an immense effort from the child but she gamely finishes it.

"That's very good, Bonnie. I enjoyed it."

"Sunday is baby Jesus' birthday."

"That's right."

"Hello again," says Kitty, laughing, pleased that all has gone so well.

"You'll try to come up, won't you, Wes?"

"Yes, I'll try, Kit."

I can hear Frank in the background telling me that I had *better* be there or he'll take a round out of me. Frank really sounds juiced. Kitty and I both chuckle.

"Good-bye, honey, and take care."

"Right, Kitty . . . thanks . . . good-bye . . ."

Sitting in the basket chair, I listen to the sound of my neighbor's television coming through the walls, a Bob Hope Christmas Special from Viet Nam. And I think about my brother Frank and the gulf that divides us. Somewhere in the middle of that gulf lies something. When our parents died there was an attempt to cross the gulf. They were killed on a foggy October night in 1957 when my father's Studebaker missed a curve on the high county road near Middlesburgh and flattened itself against an outcrop of rock. Both were killed instantly. They'd been visiting the neighborhood farms on their annual quest for winter apples and comb honey. I believe my father had a heart attack, though it was never mentioned. At the moment of their death I was drunk—lying on the floor of a friend's apartment listening to voices and laughter and the music of Miles Davis. The room was smoky and crowded when my friend came over to shake me and say there was a long-distance call. I hardly remember the car ride to Middlesburgh, only the scalding coffee which burned my lips.

At the graveside on a windy raw day I stood next to Frank. When they lowered my mother's coffin into the ground beside my father's, he squeezed my arm so hard I wanted to cry out in pain. The grey faces of the mourners swam before my eyes and the minister's words were drowned in a terrible flapping noise that came from the wind, tearing at a piece of loose tarpaulin near the grave.

That night the house was filled with relatives and friends. Both my father and Frank worked at the flour mill and they knew nearly everyone in town. And that night nearly everyone came. To pay his respects, as the saying goes. Frank had several glasses of whisky, and whenever we met in the crowded rooms, he would put his arms around me and draw me close. People stood off and watched us with approving looks.

I had a few drinks too and after wandering from room to room I stepped outside for air, stumbling through a pile of sodden leaves. It had rained earlier in the evening but now it was turning dry and cold. That infernal wind still poured down from the sky, lashing the branches of the poplars and pasting their round yellow leaves to the roofs and hoods of the cars which lined both sides of the street. I stood in front of our house and looked through the blazing windows, watching Frank move among his friends. I felt so strange, so consumed by the mystery and the wonder of it. There was really nothing to do but stand there in the windy dark street and shake my head in amazement. My father had raked these leaves a few days before. My mother had probably watched him from that very window. Now they both lay mouldering in the cold damp earth. Incredible! Our house was filled with strangers drinking coffee! Did Frank feel this mystery and this wonder too? Did anybody? Or were they all too caught up in the diversion itself? After a while I returned to the house to pack my suitcases and lie awake for several hours, listening to the voices below and thinking about the mystery and the wonder of it.

7.

It is freezing cold on the balcony tonight. The wind alone could congeal the blood. Most of the lights along the Shopping Plaza have now been turned off and the last of the clerks have walked across the parking lot to brush the snow from their cars with long wooden scrapers. Now big green trucks are being loaded by a noisy contraption which crawls around on huge tractor lugs. The wind snaps the flag on the roof of the A & P and sends swirls of snow to obscure the men who stand around the trucks smoking cigarettes.

I myself must venture forth to the Plaza one of these days, and not merely as a spectator either. After all, there are only three more shopping days left for the purchasing of

Yuletide gifts. Perhaps a stone bracelet from Mexico for Molly and a soft fuzzy bear for my son who lies tonight in Dr. Fortescue's School staring out at this snowy new world with his small hooded eyes.

8.

Although I am not particular about my television fare, *The Late Show* offerings tonight are thin indeed. Channel 4 is making much of *Miracle on Thirty-fourth Street* with Thelma Ritter and none other than Edmund (Giant Ant Killer) Gwenn. In this movie Gwenn plays the part of a department-store Santa Claus in New York City. My *TV Guide* describes *Miracle* as *a timeless and warmhearted story that makes ideal holiday viewing.* I think I can do without it.

Instead, I prefer to lie in bed and listen to the wind scream down the grey canyons of these buildings in search of the flat streets and schoolyards.

THE WEEKEND MAN

1.

I was dreaming of my father when something pulled me from sleep and left me stranded, blinking at the walls. It is three o'clock. The wind has died and left behind a cold sheer world. These buildings look so dark against the snow. Several blocks away, down Napier Avenue, I can see the flares of work crews loading trucks with snow. And coming in low over the lake the winking lights of a jet as it descends for the runway at the International Airport.

I rarely dream, and when I do, it is as often as not violent and lecherous. But tonight my dream was as tranquil and nostalgic as a glance through an old schoolbook. I was walking hand in hand with my father along a street in

Middlesburgh and I was asking him questions about the war. He was coming home from work at the flour mill, striding along with that brisk open-toed gait of his. The silver lunch pail with the black letters AW stencilled across the end was tucked squarely in the crook of his left arm. A dusting of fine white powder lay in the creases and folds of his denim jacket and along the cracks in his boots. We are talking about the British paratroopers at Arnhem in September of 1944 and where he was at the time of the battle.

My father was a weekend man, but only after he discovered that there was no other way for him to live his life. The difference between my father and most weekend men, however, was that my father chose the past quite early in his life. Many weekend men choose the past, but only after they have reached a certain age and become disenchanted with the future. My father was never much interested in the future and he chose the past when he was still a young man.

Among the best memories of my life are those childhood days when the postman delivered a letter from my father. He had joined the army a few days after Canada declared war on Germany. My mother told me about it. One September morning he went his usual way to the flour mill, but about ten-thirty he was back, sitting at the kitchen table, pouring himself a cup of coffee. My mother came in from hanging out clothes and saw him sitting there. He told her he had joined the army and if he passed the medical he would be off to Camp Borden in a few days. She was astonished.

Many people wondered why a man with a wife and two small children was so eager to join up. Some praised him for his patriotism—in fact, I got used to hearing this while I was a child. Teachers were always pointing at me in the classroom and saying things like, Wes's father is fighting for democracy. Or many of the old veterans from the First War would stop me on the street and patting my head tell me what a patriot my father was. But I don't really think my father cared all that much about his country or democracy. I think he went overseas to escape the weekender's lot, for there is no greater diversion known to man than a war on foreign soil.

He wrote beautiful letters about his life as a soldier—letters filled with the black streets of London and the awful whine of bombs in the night and the hollowed-eyed children huddled on train platforms heading north to Scotland. Sometimes he sent along bits and pieces of verse in which he described the stone churches and the green hedgerows of the countryside. There were often rooks circling high above his cornfields and great armadas of brown trucks moving along country roads in the dusk. He sounded very happy to be there looking at all this. On the eve of the invasion of Normandy, he wrote a long emotional letter, standing on the deck of a boat somewhere in the English Channel. He was very excited. *We are going to make history soon*, he wrote. *I can feel it in my bones.*

My mother read these letters to us and when she was finished she would let me hold them while I gazed in wonder at the cramped brownish writing. Afterwards I would lie on the bed in our room, watching the wind stir my brother's model airplanes—the balsa wood Spitfires and Messerschmitts, which hung by slender invisible threads from the ceiling. I would lie there, watching the planes turn slowly in the air, overwhelmed by the image of my warrior father and his battles.

When he came home, Art Wakeham disappointed many people. He disappointed my mother and the family friends because he was obviously drinking a lot and seemed in no great hurry to return to the flour mill. He disappointed Frank because the two of them discovered after a few weeks that they didn't really like each other very much. And he disappointed me too, because I was a small boy and small boys have big imaginations. It wasn't his fault that I had dreamed the dreams I had, but I blamed him anyhow, for that is the way of small boys. There is simply no room in their lives for the thundering ironies and they are only impatient with the perverseness of events.

On the day of his arrival we went to the bus terminal to meet him, the three of us nervous and ramrod stiff in our new clothes and damp hair, standing in an October day that glittered and spun like a prism before my eyes. When the bus arrived, my father was not on it. My mother walked slowly to the ticket agent's desk and was told there were no more buses that day. So we walked back to the house through that booming Ontario afternoon and solemnly ate the chicken dinner my mother had been planning for weeks.

He arrived that night shortly after dark. I heard the sound of a car motor idling outside the window and when I looked down I could see a lean dark figure standing against the car talking to the driver. They were both laughing quietly and I could see the dull glint of a bottle in the dashboard lights. Then the figure waved to the driver and picked up a long duffel bag and valise and turned towards the house. I stood there, listening to the footsteps below and my mother's muffled cry, almost swooning at the enormity of the event.

And what of this modern Ulysses—this great romantic adventurer and writer of magic journals now returned to hearth and family? When he entered my room and switched on the light, he turned out to be a thin tired-looking man in rumpled khaki with sour breath and the faint smell of public washrooms about him. The dark hair fell across his brow in a boyish forelock and the big ingenuous eyes and shy grin made him look not much older than Frank. He didn't really look like anybody's father, let alone mine, and when he bent forward to kiss me I felt the most acute disappointment.

Now Captain Art Wakeham was back from the foreign war. He stored away his uniform in an upstairs closet and put on grey slacks and a glen check jacket. Then he quietly drifted into a deep malaise like a ship becalmed in the doldrum waters. After the first few weeks he spoke only when addressed and for months he sat at the kitchen table, unfailingly polite, yet staring glumly out the window at the snow which fell day after day from the heavy gunmetal skies. He sat there bemused until the milky suns of late March melted the ice and the robins returned to perch outside the window and cock a weather eye at him. And all through this period of dry-eyed funk my mother wrung her hands and said nothing. My brother Frank stayed away from the house most of the time and when he was home he kept to himself in our room.

Meanwhile, I asked endless questions about the war and the great events he lived through. My father never mentioned the war to anyone but me. But with me he would talk about the particular Thursday he saw his first German soldier, or how he felt on a certain Wednesday in London after the bombers had left and he found himself still alive. He was always careful about the time and day, and I suspect he kept a diary, though no one ever saw it. He would look across the table at me and then out the window and say: Now this happened on Monday, September 22, 1944, at about two-thirty in the afternoon. Or: That is how I felt at around five-twenty on the morning of Thursday, August 19, 1942. Then he would work out the time difference between London or wherever and Middlesburgh, and I would get busy imagining what I had been doing at that precise moment. It became something of a game with us—my favourite childhood game.

In the later stages of his Great Malaise, my father took long walks, wandering the winter streets of the town, oblivious to the housewives who stared at him from behind their curtains or the delivery men who watched his absent manner with narrow averted glances. Most people believed my father suffered shell shock in the war and they rarely looked him in the eye. Towards spring his walks became more frequent and sometimes he would go beyond the town limits and tramp across the fields of tough brown grass which stretch down to the shores of the bay. Or he would stride along the gummy township roads under the spring sky like a medieval friar, watching the blackbirds career down the swift air—stopping now and then with a stick to gauge the depth and current of a roadside brook. I followed him once on one of these mysterious pilgrimages, hiding behind trees to watch him climb the rail fences and stand in someone's meadow, watching and listening, for what?

One April evening he returned from a walk in a jubilant mood. The change in his nature was so dramatic that my mother and I both looked at each other. Frank was away. My father didn't seem to notice our surprise. He was fiercely excited by something. And he was cold sober.

"God, what an evening!" he said, sitting down and looking around at us. His face was flushed and his big zircon eyes sparkled and blazed. He just sat there for a few moments, shaking his dark head and looking at us wonderingly. His entire body seemed to tremble with some secret thrilling pleasure.

"Look," he said finally, "I know it sounds crazy, but let's the three of us walk to Summit Hill."

My mother was standing near the stove watching him. She was gradually recovering from her amazement and with each passing moment was gathering new strength. His suggestion was like nothing I had heard on earth before.

"Really now." He laughed like a child and placed the palms of his hands flat on the table. "It's very simple. It's such a fine evening. We'll be back in a couple of hours."

"But I'm cooking dinner, Art," my mother said matter-of-factly. "It's almost done."

My father frowned at this and drummed his fingers along the table. "Well . . . it'll keep, won't it? Come on now!"

My mother lifted a pot from the stove and took it to the sink, where she drained off the water from the potatoes. The steam rose to fog the glass above the counter. She carefully shook down the potatoes, looking into the pot as if she half-expected to find something other than the steaming vegetables there.

"Well, what do you say now?" he asked, looking over at her.

"Oh, Art, what are you thinking of?" she said. "It'll be dark soon." Then she brightened and walked across the room. "Let's plan for Sunday, eh! We can go on Sunday if the weather holds."

"I don't want to go on Sunday, goddam it, I want to go now," he said slowly. "I might be dead on Sunday, we might all be dead."

My mother's eyes flashed with anger.

"Don't talk such foolishness, for heaven's sakes," she said. "What are you talking about, dead? What are you trying to do? Frighten this child to death?"

"It's not foolishness," he answered, and suddenly they were at each other. The long winter's frustration was erupting at last into furious boil. My mother may not have been able to cope with his terrible silences and the dreamy abstracted afternoons by the window, but she could handle fury and tumult with the best of them.

"You'd better pull yourself together, Mister," she said coldly.

"I am together," he shouted. "Don't you worry about that."

"I worry about it," she said. "I have to worry about it. Nobody else around here seems to be doing any worrying."

"Oh Christ, what do you want from me?" He was shaking like a leaf.

"What do I want from you?" my mother cried like an actress. The question was outrageous. "I want you to act like a husband and father. I want you to pull yourself together and stop spending all your time day-dreaming about overseas. The war is finished now and I'm asking you to understand that fact."

"I understand it. I understand it." He was on his feet, trembling with rage, almost in tears. Then he bolted for the door and was gone, disappearing into his fine April evening.

He came home very late and very drunk. I heard him shuffling around downstairs and after a few moments I could smell the cigarette smoke rising from his lonely vigil by the kitchen window. The next day, though, he was up and gone before any of us were awake. When he came back at noon he was carrying a brown paper parcel. After lunch he unwrapped the parcel, dressed himself in the stiff new denim smock, and walked out the door to the flour mill.

Until his death eleven and a half years later my father never missed a single working day in his life. Nor did he and my mother ever raise angry voices to each other again.

After he had settled into work, the Great Malaise disappeared, never to return. If you imagine for a moment that he lapsed into some kind of sullen martyrdom, you are wrong. My father was no constant sufferer. He turned out to be a quiet calm soul whom most people took for a deep thinker, though I don't believe he thought deeply about anything except the great events he once lived through.

He abandoned the long walks and bought himself a small grey Studebaker, a low-slung vehicle of revolutionary design. Or so it seemed in 1947. Each Saturday morning, fair weather or foul, he washed and vacuumed it with great care. In fact, for the rest of his life my father became a man of tidy and regular habits. People could set their watches by his movements and I think he took a certain pleasure in this. He drank only a few bottles of beer at Christmas and gave up cigarettes in 1948. For his own good reasons he refused to mingle with the other veterans at the local Legion and he never talked to me again about the war. Nor did we play any more at our special game.

There were times, though, when I knew he was thinking about things and having a little diversion all his own. He might be sitting in a chair reading the newspaper or listening to the radio, but his eyes would glaze over and he would sink his tongue into one corner of his cheek, like a man who has momentarily lost his way in a strange city and is trying to puzzle things out. Then he was away from all of us, playing back the old reels, having a fine time.

2.

This morning the sunlight dances off the snow and makes the eyes water. Below my window the whine of spinning tires burns the air as some unfortunate worker begins his Thursday in a snowbank, up to his frozen ballocks in the white stuff and already late for the meetings and decisions.

I breakfast on Rice Krispies, whole-wheat toast, and Instant Sanka, the luck of the draw. On the counter of my kitchenette are two glass jars formerly holding Peter Pan Peanut Butter. Now each contains several slips of paper. One jar is lettered "Breakfast Menus" and the other, "Routes to the Office." Each weekday morning I close my eyes and draw forth one piece of paper from each jar. I have about a dozen breakfast menus in the one: simple meals like Special "K" with cracked-wheat toast and cocoa, boiled egg, English muffin and tea, Banana Instant Breakfast—things like that. If I didn't leave my choice to the impersonal decisions of Chance, I know I would end up doing what my father did every working day of his life: sitting down before a bowl of cornflakes and two pieces of white toast. And I know that sooner or later this would sneak up and get me in strange ways.

The same with going to work. I have laid out eighteen routes to the office—some of them quite tricky, involving dead-end crescents and one-way streets. It can take me anything from five minutes to half an hour to get to work in the morning, depending on which piece of paper I draw from the peanut-butter jar. The shortest and most direct way, of course, is along Union Avenue to Britannia Road and north for a few blocks—the route I travel homeward each evening. The half-hour trip which I have called the Jumbo Route is a knotty criss-cross affair in which I avoid all the big avenues and take to the back streets of Union Place, always watching carefully for the little children who sometimes disobey Elmer the Safety Elephant and dart out from behind parked cars. I've only drawn the Jumbo once since I started working at Winchester House.

3.

As I enter Winchester House on this white and blue morning, I can sense something electric in the atmosphere. There is an undercurrent of aliveness behind the noise of billing machines and typewriters. The very air crackles and smokes with it. The faces behind the machines are more animated; the eyes are more wary and alert. There is a large diversion in the air. This is not bad for a Thursday; in fact, it's unusually good—what I call a double diversion. As if the tinkle and tinsel of Christmas were not enough, there is also this new expectation. I, too, am secretly thrilled by it all and my first thoughts are of death. Someone important has died. Harry Ingram has had a heart attack in New York or Sydney

Calhoun has keeled over at his desk. Perhaps Cecil White has jumped from the washroom window and landed on his neck. Even Mrs. Bruner's stony Teutonic face betrays some inner life today. We nod to each other, unsmiling and correct. I get on better with her when I assume brisk ways, so today I will be civil, though distant and icy, Frau Bruner. Through the open door to Sydney's office I can see Roger MacCarthy's heavy bulk in grey slacks and blue blazer. He is leaning against the Territory Board with his hands in his trouser pockets, talking to Sydney and rocking back and forth on the heels of his wide shoes. Ron Tuttle is in there too: I can hear his nervous laughter from time to time. Oh, something is definitely astir!

On my desk is the morning mail—the usual begging letters requesting complimentary copies. Teachers hate to buy books. I don't blame them. Here is an irate letter full of righteousness and injured feelings from Mr. Wilbur Goodlow, principal of Eagle High. He would like to know why he has not seen a representative from Winchester House since Mr. Hickman called on him, whoever he was. I believe now someone told me he was my predecessor, twice removed. Sydney has scrawled a message across the top of this letter: *This is your territory Wes. What about it? Better see him early in the New Year. And write now to that effect. Copy of letter to me, please.* Right! I will do that this moment but Roger MacCarthy stands in the doorway, grinning in at me.

"Hey, Wes! How's it going?"

I look up in mock surprise and smile. "Morning, Roger."

The big fellow eyes me cagily as he roams about my office in his restless way, stirring the change in his pockets, thumbing through the sample copies on my bookshelf, and waiting for me to say: What's new, Rog?

"So what's new, Rog?" I ask, looking up.

"Syd got a call from New York this morning," he says cryptically.

"Oh!"

Roger flicks a particle of dust from the cover of *Learning Language Skills* and looks over at me.

"We've been sold, Wes, old buddy."

"How's that?"

"Sold. S-O-L-D. Fairfax Press, Winchester House, the whole kit and caboodle has been bought up by Uke." Roger is fantastically agitated by all this and can't keep still for a second.

"Uke?" I ask.

"Yes. U-E-C, Universal Electronics Corporation. Harry is flying home tonight and will address the staff tomorrow on the details of the sale and where we fit into all this. According to Syd, Harry sounded pretty depressed by it all, though it's hard to say where this will leave any of us."

Roger tells all this quickly, like a small child describing a serious accident down the street. Now he stops to dig deeply into one pocket, scratching a ball, no doubt.

"What do you think, Wes?"

"About what, Rog?"

"About this sale. The whole shebang."

"I don't know. It's a corker, isn't it?" I shake my head to please him.

"You're so right," he says, shaking *his* head now. "I can't say that I'd care to be in old Syd's shoes."

"Why is that?"

Roger crosses to the door and closes it softly. He then walks back and leaning forward spreads a thick buttock across one corner of my desk.

"Listen," he whispers, "from what I've heard the boys at Uke don't horse around."

"Yes?"

"They've no time for inferior performances."

"No?"

"It could mean a lot more pressure on all of us."

"Yes?"

"Yes. Listen." Roger leans further forward. I can smell the last syrupy traces of Scope mouthwash on his breath. I am a Scope user myself. "I've heard we've had a pretty bad fall, saleswise."

"I see."

"Don't breathe a word of this, but Ron had lunch the other day with John Derbyshire in Accounting. They're like this, you know."

Roger lifts both hands, curling the middle fingers over the forefingers to demonstrate the snug relationship between Ron Tuttle and John Derbyshire.

"John told him that sales for October and November weren't exactly inspiring."

I manage a weak smile. "Doesn't say much for us, eh!"

Roger doesn't find this amusing. Instead, he looks at me with a heavy frown. This narrows and darkens his brow and makes him look like a dull child. He picks up the porcelain ball paperweight from my desk and hefts it in one hand.

"Wes . . . we may all be under the gun, you know," he says, smiling grimly.

Although I do not say so, the prospect of being under the gun, as Roger puts it, does not much move me one way or another. All I can do is observe that Roger seems to enjoy the prospect of being under the gun, and if this tiny drop of fear injected into his system is helping to make his day, I am all for it.

"I just wouldn't want to be in Syd's shoes, that's all," he says again, shaking his head.

"No, I suppose not."

Roger has had a fresh haircut and the back of his head is bristly. When he bends forward I can see the patch of white at the exact centre of his scalp. Roger will have a bald head one day. His wrestler's neck is beginning to overtake the collars of his broadcloth shirts. Nearly every day after lunch when he is in the office, Roger unbuttons his collar and loosens his tie so that he looks like a city detective who has been grilling a suspect for hours. Now, though, the soft collar looks filled to the point of bursting. Roger strokes my porcelain ball in a peculiarly suggestive manner, rubbing a broad thumb across its lambent surface.

"Anyway," he says, standing up and placing the ball on my desk, "we'll know soon enough, I guess."

"That's true," I agree.

He moves towards the door, calling over his shoulder. "Say, Wes . . . how about joining Ron and me for lunch today? We're going over to The Skipper's Table."

"Good idea, Rog. Yes, I'd like that."

"Right."

"Okay now, bye."

"Bye, bye."

After Roger leaves I make a start on my letter to Wilbur Goodlow of Eagle High. *Dear Mr. Goodlow: Thank you for your letter of December 17. We are sorry not to have called on you before this, but staff changes have necessitated a reorganization and—*I tear it up with a groan and think of Molly. This is not a good time of the year for the major decisions, Molly. The Christian world is topsy-turvy during these last days of the old year. There is too much peppermint in the air and I cannot think straight. Let us wrestle our problems to standstill. I am all for that. But let us do it on some commonplace Monday in January when the world has been scrubbed clean and we can see more clearly what's what.

4.

"Hello, Harold. No . . . of course, you're not bothering me. And I'm sorry not to have returned your call yesterday, but I got tied up in a sales meeting . . ."

I am telling innocent lies to Harold Pendle, who is calling me between periods from Union Place Secondary School. In the background I can hear milling voices and the trumpeting blare of a loudspeaker which is informing everyone within three miles that there will be an assembly in the school auditorium this afternoon at three o'clock.

"I hope I haven't called you at an inopportune time," Harold says in his reedy voice. "I'm calling from the general office."

"No, Harold, as a matter of fact I was on the point . . ."

". . . Thursday is a difficult day for me, as I have teaching periods straight through until number seven and no *spares*."

"That sounds rough."

"Yes, it is."

There is a long pause during which both of us claw frantically at our minds for a phrase or two. Harold finally catches hold of one.

"I'm having some friends in tonight . . . a small pre-holiday get-together. They're mostly teachers, though one or two are from the business world like yourself. . . . I know it's awfully late, but I was wondering if you would be free to join us . . ." I am not going to enjoy myself at Harold Pendle's pre-holiday get-together. I don't even particularly like Harold Pendle, and I don't think he particularly likes me either. But I think I will go, nevertheless. After all, it is the holiday season: a time to make merry. I haven't been invited to a party for months, perhaps it's years now. Frankly I can't remember my last party.

"Well, Harold, this is very good of you. . . . Yes, as a matter of fact, I would be free to join you tonight and I'd love to come . . ."

Another great crackle and the booming voice of the loudspeaker rumbles through the wires into my ears. *May I have your attention, please. May I have your attention, please. Due to Miss Bonheimer's illness, French classes for 9c, 9f, 10c, and 11e have been cancelled for today. Students in these classes are hereby instructed to proceed to the Cafeterium for a study period at the scheduled time. To repeat, due to Miss Bonheimer's illness . . .*

Again there is heavy silence between Harold and me. He must also be listening to the loudspeaker's message about Miss Bonheimer's illness . . .

"Hello. Hello, Harold?"

"What?"

"Hello."

"Yes?"

"I'd like to come tonight."

"Good. That's fine. I'm sorry but I just wanted to catch that message. It seems that one of the staff is ill today. We've been hit pretty hard lately by the flu bug."

"Yes. Well, it's the season for it all right."

"Pardon?"

"I say, it is the season for flu all right."

"Oh, yes. Yes, it is that . . . Well, I'm glad you can come tonight. Any time after eight will be fine. Do you know where I live?"

"No, I'm afraid not."

"I see. Do you know Union Place at all?"

"Oh, yes, and I have a good map."

"Well, fine. There should be no problem then. . . I live at eleven-forty . . . do you have a pencil there?"

"Yes, go ahead."

"Eleven-forty-seven Union Park Crescent . . . it's the last house on the street . . . a white colonial. You really can't miss it."

"Fine."

"There's a large Santa Claus on the roof."

"Yes?"

"For the children, you know."

"Oh, of course."

"The words Season's Greetings flash off and on. You can't miss that."

"Right you are."

There is another awkward pause during which I hear someone ask for five hundred sheets of foolscap and Billy

Butler's attendance record. Billy is in 9d. Harold sounds pained.

"Um, I wonder, will your wife be coming along? She's quite welcome, you know."

"No, I think not, Harold. I'll be coming alone."

"I see. Well, suit yourself. It's just that Edna likes to have this sort of information beforehand. It helps her to plan the food."

"Of course."

The deafening blast of a bell sounds alarum in my ears. Harold must be leaning on it.

"There's the bell. I'm afraid I have to run. We'll look for you tonight. Anytime after eight. Eleven-forty-seven Union Park Crescent. The house with Season's Greetings on the roof."

"Right, and thank you, Harold."

"You're welcome. Good-bye."

Harold Pendle and I were classmates at old Middlesburgh High back in the middle fifties. We had nothing in common and probably said not fifty words to each other through five years of high school. To tell the truth, I always found him a bit priggish, sitting in his straight-backed way, up near the front of the room with the girls. He was a teacher's favourite—a Queen's Scout and a straight-A student. Before examinations, while many of us moaned darkly about failure, Harold would sit at his desk with his hands folded in front of him, waiting for the signal to begin. He seemed to relish these tests and examinations.

Victories over Harold were always small and cheap. In the liniment air of the locker room he was often crudely persecuted by people like Weiner Collins. Weiner was an oaf really, a squat bullet-headed tackle on the football team whose idea of humour was to mince around the locker room stark naked, twitching a huge and hairy ass in an exaggeratedly effeminate manner. It always broke us up. My brother Frank has told me that Weiner is now an alderman on the Middlesburgh town council, but in those days he liked nothing better than to torment Harold Pendle in the locker room of old Middlesburgh High. One of his favourite games was to wait until Harold was seated on the bench in front of his locker squirming into his striped shorts. Weiner then liked to walk across the room and stand next to Harold naked as a baby. From there he would carry on some lewd conversation with another football player across the room while he lifted a fat leg to the bench, thus allowing his sizeable meat to swing freely, inches from Harold's nose. Sometimes, though not often, I felt sorry for Harold Pendle.

After high school, Harold took Honours English at Queen's University and, from what I heard, married the brightest girl in his class before settling down to teach at Union Place Secondary School. During those years I saw him only once or twice in Middlesburgh. Once in front of Loblaws on a broiling July day I watched him load a Ford station wagon with parcels—a tall spindle-legged figure in white shorts, tee shirt, and sneakers. A young horse-faced woman sat on the front seat of the wagon frowning out at the hot street while two small girls crawled over the groceries. Harold was busy with his parcels and never looked up as I walked by. I didn't think I knew him well enough to say hello. Another time a couple of years later, a man who looked very much like Harold nodded to me gravely from the front seat of a station wagon as it went by on a wet Sunday afternoon in August. But the windows of the car were steamed up and I couldn't be sure it was Harold.

Beyond those two occasions, I never saw Harold Pendle again until one Wednesday morning in September when I visited Union Place Secondary School. It was a warm hazy day, one of the last days of summer. On my way into the school I stopped for a moment near the door to savour the fine morning and watch a class of girls stretch through some calisthenics on the athletic field. They were handsome young fillies, Grade Tenners; all smooth brown legs and arms sticking every which way from sky-blue jumpers. Their leader was a short woman in a white gym suit with close-cropped hair and muscular legs, a shot-putter for sure. She kept blowing the little silver whistle around her neck and with each shrill blast those lovely brown berries of girls would unlimber a new set of muscles to the sun. I confess that I might have stood there dreaming away that sweet young flesh until empires crumbled, but a voice from behind startled me into wakefulness.

"Pretty nice stuff, eh!" the voice said maliciously. "You could go to jail for what you're thinking, my friend."

I turned in some amazement. The speaker was a round-shouldered sandy-haired little man in his middle forties. Now he stood there next to me, slapping a worn briefcase against his trouser leg and staring across the athletic field through speckle-rimmed glasses.

"I've been looking at it five days a week for fifteen years," he said, shaking his head slowly. "Believe me, you never get used to it." He noisily sucked a tooth. "And this is the worst time of all. The little twats . . . they come back from the summer all tanned and sweet . . . wearing those frickin' short skirts . . ." He suddenly gave me a broad wink and dug me in the ribs with his elbow, like a man at a stag party. "Listen, my friend. Sometimes it's so bad I can't get up from my desk . . . I don't dare . . ."

"Yes?"

He grinned and leered like a music-hall comic. "You know, eh?"

"How do you mean?"

He looked around and then jerked a forefinger towards his fly. "Can't keep her down sometimes, so help me."

"Oh yes," I laughed weakly. The man was a maniac for sure.

"And don't think some of them don't want it too."

He leaned forward and gripped my arm with firm surprising strength. "Lots of them are *begging* for it," he said, threateningly.

He stood back now and looked me squarely in the eye for the first time. "You a salesman, my friend?"

"Yes."

"Well then, you know what I mean, eh!" he snorted, digging me in the ribs again. I nodded, wondering how to escape from this lunatic man. He quickly stuck out a hand.

"The name's Hank Bellamy. I'm Chem Head here. Have you got anything new in organic for the five-year A & S's?"

"Well . . ."

He glanced at the watch on his lean freckled wrist. "Keerist . . . I'm frickin' near late as it is . . . We'll be talking to you now, eh . . ."

"Wakeham . . . Wes Wakeham . . ."

"Right, Wes, we'll see you now . . ."

And he was gone, spinning through the heavy door like a top, leaving me to my search for the Men Teachers' Lounge.

I had an appointment that morning with the head of the Biology Department and I was seated in a large chair by a window waiting for him when a tall thin man entered the lounge. He was ramrod straight with stiff reddish hair, a jutting Adam's apple, and a narrow prim face which looked oddly familiar to me. He glanced over once or twice while he poured a cup of coffee from a large chromium urn.

The lounge itself gave off a pleasant hum of murmuring

voices and quiet laughter. Most of the teachers were relaxing, smoking their pipes and cigarettes, talking about the summer and waiting for the next period to begin. The atmosphere was clubby and restrained. The morning sun slanted through the venetian blinds, and dusty bars of yellow light played along the carpet and leather chairs. I began to feel drowsy; in my memory the raving man was retreating before the idiot beat of sunlight on my left temple. In an heroic attempt to stay awake, I thumbed through *The Chain of Life*, which lay heavy and lumpish in my lap.

Through half-closed eyelids, I watched the tall thin man approach my chair, a meagre smile on his face. The book lay open to a three-colour illustration depicting the metamorphosis of *Adalia bipunctata* or ladybird beetle. The tall man spoke to me in this reedy voice.

"Hello, there . . . Don't I know you . . ."

"Why. . . !"

"Would your name be Wes Wakeham by any chance?"

"Why, yes." I said, struggling to my feet. "And you're . . ."

"Harold Pendle," he said, offering me a slender hand as cold as ice.

"Of course . . . How are you, Harold?"

"Well, thank you," he said, still smiling thinly. "I see you're in the selling business now . . . " He sat down carefully in a chair and held his cup of coffee in one hand. "Which company do you represent, by the way?"

"I'm with Winchester House."

"Ah, yes! I believe I've met one of your men at one time or another . . . Calhoun . . . I think that was the name . . ."

He paused to sip his coffee, looking at me over the rim of his cup. "The last time I heard about you, you were working for an advertising agency or something . . ."

"Yes, though that was some time ago."

Harold sipped the hot coffee slowly, taking care not to burn his lips. "I see," he said finally. "Anyway, I'm extremely sorry to hear of your misfortune."

"What's that?" I asked.

Harold placed his coffee cup on the floor and lighted a king-size cigarette. "Your son. I've heard about his condition and I'm very sorry. I hope this doesn't embarrass you. I believe in being totally frank about these things."

"Yes. Yes. Good idea . . ."

He puffed his cigarette rapidly and waited several seconds before speaking again.

"So how long have you been in this line?"

"Oh, just a couple of weeks," I said. "I'm just a rookie actually."

"I see," Harold said. "Well . . . I'll be glad to take a look at what you have to offer, though I think it only fair to warn you that we've already made our appropriations for the coming year. Still, there's always next year, isn't there?"

"I hope so . . ."

"What?"

"Nothing."

"It's never too soon to prepare for that."

"Yes," I said, dully.

"Mr. MacCauley depends on our advice in choosing texts and materials. He's one *head* who takes the advice of his teachers, thank heaven. And, after all, why not? We are the ones who have to work with the material."

"That's true."

Now he pulled his chair closer and leaned forward like an old maid, resting his hands on bony knees.

"Would your firm be interested in publishing a new kind of grammar text?" he asked, *sotto voce*.

"Well, yes. I imagine we would, Harold."

"You *imagine* you would," he said testily.

"Well . . . it's difficult to say . . . without knowing more."

"I see. Yes, fair enough," he said, leaning back in the heavy leather chair. It hissed softly under his weight.

He looked at me with a frown and then leaned forward again. "I've had this project in mind for a couple of years and now I believe I'm prepared to approach a publisher about it." He puffed quickly on the long cigarette. "*Reflexive Grammar for Today!* How does that sound?"

"It sounds fine to me."

"It's a totally new approach to the teaching of grammar and frankly I'm excited about it. I've talked to one or two of my colleagues and they like what they hear too . . . though, mind you, it's still rather secretive." He paused and gave me a stern look. "Do you really think your firm might be interested?"

"Yes . . . yes, I do, Harold."

"I've done quite a bit of research. I have several folders of notes. Twenty to be exact, though I haven't started the actual writing."

I began to see a way out of this.

"I understand. Well, now look, Harold. Why not send along a sample chapter and outline? Send it to me. Then I can show it to the editors."

He paused to tap his lips with a long finger. "Yes, good idea," he said, looking down at the long grey ash on his cigarette. "Yes, indeed. That sounds sensible . . . a sample chapter and outline."

He tapped the ash into the saucer. "By the way," he added, "do you people have American connections?"

"Oh, yes. We're associated with Fairfax Press in New York. And London."

"Excellent. My personal opinion is that this book could

have . . . I emphasize could have . . . considerable relevance to the American senior-high-school market."

"Wonderful."

He bent down for his coffee cup. "Well, Wakeham, I'm very glad we had this opportunity to chat. Let's hope that it proves . . . mutually . . . rewarding . . ."

"You bet."

"When I came in I just happened to look across the room and saw you sitting here. And I said to myself, that looks an awful lot like a chap I went to school with."

"I'm glad we had this talk too, Harold."

"And you think a chapter and outline is the way to handle it?"

"Absolutely yes . . . it's by far the most professional approach and nearly all of our more established authors do this. You see, it gives the editors an opportunity to assess the project at all levels . . ." I was really warming up.

"Quite. I see that now, yes. Well, fine then, I'll see that you get these in the very near future."

He stood up, straightening his long lean frame like a jack-in-the-box. We shook hands.

"It was very nice to have seen you again, Wakeham. I don't expect you get back to Middlesburgh very often now."

"No. Just once or twice a year to see my brother and his family."

"I see. And how is your wife?"

"She's just fine, thank you."

"Good. Well then, I'll be in touch with you. Meanwhile, if there is anyone here in the room I can introduce you to . . ." He waved a languid arm around the lounge.

"No, no . . . That's fine, Harold," I said, thrusting my business card into his hand, the low point in a salesman's day. "Our address."

"Ah, good. Thank you."

I watched him walk across the room to put his coffee cup on a small table near the urn—the same pigeon-toed, slightly mincing steps which had once taken him to the blackboards of old Middlesburgh High to work out some impossible problem in geometry. He stopped for a moment to talk to another teacher and then headed for the door. As he went through the doorway he stepped aside to admit the mad Bellamy, who spun through clutching an armful of papers. Bellamy stood at the urn pouring himself a cup of coffee and looking around the room. He spied me almost immediately and grinned. From where he was standing, no one except myself could see him and he took this opportunity to make a circle with the thumb and forefinger of one hand. Then he rapidly poked the forefinger of his other hand through the circle several times and gave me a broad wink into the bargain. An odd fellow, certainly!

Harold Pendle's sample chapter and outline arrived on my desk a couple of weeks later. I glanced through it but I know nothing about the mechanics of grammar and anyway it bores me half to death. So I cannot tell you much about Harold's grammar book. I sent the material along with a memorandum to Sydney Calhoun and I've heard nothing about it since. I know that Sydney's memorandum folder is crammed these days and it's unlikely he'll get around to reading it and passing the stuff along to Cecil White for some time. When Harold calls, I am always careful to tell the truth and explain that everything is still under consideration and that as far as we're concerned the project is still feasible.

5.

Today the Shopping Plaza is crowded with sleek well-dressed women, some of whom push children around the Mall in little silver and red strollers supplied free by the Plaza: *"Another Shoppers' Service From Union Plaza,"* as it says along the sides of the strollers. It's lunch hour and nearly everyone is trying to squeeze into the restaurant for a bite before resuming their Christmas shopping. It's not surprising that in the stress of the hour the serving people should appear flushed and irritable. A few moments ago I overheard a waiter cursing in his teeth as he left the table across from us. Seated around the table are several women; solid 150-pounders in tartan tam-o'-shanters, slacks, and woollen pullovers. They've just come in from the curling rink and now they're having a drink before lunch. Away from their husbands and children, they are boisterous and giddy as school girls. They appear to be enjoying some huge private joke with endless variations and codas. Another whispered remark around the table sends them reeling into laughter. Their leader is a big handsome woman with grey-blue hair. She could be a doctor's wife—an organizer of bazaars and rummage sales. She looks like a good sport, one who can throw a fair stone or sit under the plaid blanket on chilly autumn Saturdays and cheer for the colours. She is trying to maintain order but her heart is not really in it. She is like a teacher on the last day of school: there is too much fun going on here. She scans the menu, looking wise and severe with her smart fluted reading glasses well down her nose. Then someone makes another crack and this sets them off again. Now the big woman lifts the glasses from her nose and lets them fall across her chest, where they hang suspended by a slender gold chain. She laughs right along with the rest of them, shaking her fine head and saying: Now girls. They are having a grand time, these Union Place housewives.

Roger MacCarthy, Ron Tuttle, and I are seated by one of the port holes at The Skipper's Table. We are enjoying our Seven Seas Rumpots and looking at the ladies. The Skipper's Table is expensive and smart and usually I wouldn't be here but eating the Thursday Special at the Woolworth's lunch counter. Tomorrow was to have been my day to break the luncheon pattern for this week. I was planning to have two Zumburgers and a glass of milk at the Zumburger stand in the Arcade. I may still do this. Ron Tuttle seldom goes out for lunch. Ron just bought a house in Union Place and money is tight so he brings his sandwiches to the office in little plastic wrappers called Baggies. But jolly Roger has persuaded both of us to live it up in honour of the season.

The Skipper's Table has been built to resemble the captain's quarters in an old sailing vessel. It has great oak beams along the ceiling and oval-shaped portholes for windows. We are sitting in what is known as The Poop: a small raised gallery along one side of the dining room next to the bar. The smoky yellow lighting comes from electric lanterns along the walls and the heavy dark tables are covered with pewter mugs and pitchers. In the background above the murmur of voices and rattling dishes you can hear the stirring sound of old sea chanteys. The waiters are roguish-looking fellows in striped jerseys and bell-bottom pants. The maître d' is a beauty: a tall red-faced and regal-looking man in a captain's uniform, complete with gold braid and a three-cornered hat. When I first came here several months ago with Molly he met us at the door with the words "Welcome aboard!" I've noticed, however, that he no longer greets people in this way. Now he merely nods and escorts you to your table, walking ahead very stiff and erect like some large remarkable bird.

Roger is feeling buoyant today and is looking forward to tomorrow afternoon when the staff at Winchester House will have a small Christmas party in the general office. Roger is hoping that after a few drinks girls like Shirley Pendergast will grow all warm and friendly and move their hips in a certain way. Roger is probably dreaming of a few feels behind the filing cabinet. He's having an excellent time looking forward to all this merriment and maid-chasing.

Ron Tuttle is smiling craftily and looking around the room at the people. He has just been telling us about his plans to finish the basement over the holidays. He has struck a bargain on plywood siding and is very high on a local dealer. The three of us are smiling and spooning clam chowder into our mouths, looking for all the world like three young go-ahead businessmen discussing the morning market. And truth to tell, it does feel good to be sitting here among these prosperous and well-groomed people drinking from my Seven Seas Rumpot and spooning clam chowder into my mouth. There is much to be said for the good steady grind and a new Pontiac in the spring and a Hi Bill over the back fence of a Saturday morning and a little pension at the end.

"So what do you think about the big sale, Wes?" Ron asks, guiding his spoon carefully around his chowder bowl.

"Hell, I don't really know what to think, Ron," I say enthusiastically. "I guess I'm still too green to guess."

Roger pops another roll into his mouth and mills it quickly between grindstone teeth.

"Well, let's face it," he says, swallowing dryly. "There's bound to be some changes. They'll probably send some efficiency expert up to look over the whole operation. We'll all have to be on our toes."

"That's probably true," I offer helpfully.

Roger leaves our fate hanging in the air while he struggles with the question of whether to consume the last roll. The inner conflict makes him frown darkly into the wicker breadbasket. Ron solves his problem by neatly plucking the roll and breaking it over his plate in crumbly pieces.

"What do *you* think of Syd as sales manager, Wes?" Ron asks, buttering a piece of roll with small deft strokes.

"Oh, Syd's all right, I suppose. He knows a lot of people in the business and he has lots of energy."

"Syd's a wonderful guy but he has no ideas," Roger says. "He's not an original thinker."

Ron laughs at this, a mirthless little laugh.

"That may be true, Rog," I say, "but it seems to me that knowing the right people is just as important. Or am I wrong about this?" I shrug. "After all, I'm just new."

"Oh, sure, it's very important," Roger says.

"You don't seem to consider originality all that important in educational publishing, Wes," Ron says, smiling.

"Now, I didn't quite say that, Ron."

But Ron is angry as a jay and munches his roll, fiercely smiling at the keg-shaped salt and pepper shakers.

"Excuse me, Wes," he says, "but I think that after you've been in the business a little longer you'll realize that there is a little more to it than just knowing the right people."

He looks up and flashes me a brilliant smile.

"I've absolutely no doubt of that, Ron," I say.

Roger doesn't notice Ron's annoyance but looks instead across the room where the maître d' is seating a tall blond girl.

"Look at that now, Wes," he whispers, eyeing the blonde like a Roman. "Pretty nice stuff, eh!"

"Oh my, yes! Isn't that something now?"

The curling ladies are busy with their tuna salads and the waiter brings our Davy Jones Specials, laying the plates of seafood before us with a sullen mutinous look. In a mood of mischief I order another round of Seven Seas Rumpots and trade jokes with Roger. Ron smiles thinly through it all, showing me his small perfect teeth.

After lunch Roger MacCarthy and I make our way across the parking lot of Union Place Shopping Plaza. Ron Tuttle has hurried off to buy a shirt for his father-in-law who is staying with them over the winter. As we trudge along I watch a small bird-like woman manoeuvre her husband's Cadillac between two cars. She is having trouble fitting it into the space. On the seat beside her, a little boy with the same sharp features is spinning his toy steering-wheel. On his face is that rapt look of small children at serious play. The woman has backed the big car into the space at a bad angle and in correcting it she lightly touches the fender of one of the cars. The Caddy's gleaming rear bumper neatly scrapes against a frisky looking Karman Ghia, carving out a thin white scar on the little coupés ultra-marine fender. The woman glances out at me with a weak smile. I smile back and walk on. I want my smile to say: *It is nothing to me, fellow traveller.* I think it does. When I look back, she has left the space and is already nosing the Cadillac into another, stretching her long neck like a snake to peer over the steering wheel.

The effects of the Seven Seas Rumpots are beginning to wear away and both Roger and I are on the point of feeling sluggish and let down. The gloom is settling on our shoulders like chimney soot. Roger tramps on ahead of me, his big back muscles hunched up in the pile coat. The sky has clouded over and a stiff little breeze stirs the loose snow into eddies at our feet. The traffic moves smoothly along Britannia Road, throwing up a splatter of mud along the banked sides, which now are covered with an evil-looking black crust.

What is going on here anyway? We are both well fed and clothed and living in the land of the free. Why does this sour Monday morning gloom come sifting down on the wind of Britannia Road this winter afternoon? The weekend is only hours away and I am sunk in despair.

At the corner of Britannia Road and Belvedere, directly in front of the E-con-o-mart, Roger and I stop for a red light. And here I stand, watching the traffic stream through the intersection, praying for a diversion, perhaps a small property accident, one in which people climb from their cars, death-pale and shaken by it all.

6.

A few moments ago Mrs. Bruner looked in and asked me
if I would like more tea. I shook my head and said no, looking as stern as a Prussian general. This tough no-nonsense
relationship is working. She is behaving herself. Perhaps this
is the way to conduct one's life. Adopt a firm and unsmiling
approach to people and events; be on top of every situation
Monday to Sunday. Walk proudly like the Black Panther
people, a look on the face which says to one and all: I am
taking no bullshit now, so watch your step! My telephone
is ringing.

"Mr. Wakeham . . . it's Lois Teale at the Fortescue . . ."

"Yes, Mrs. Teale. Is anything the matter?"

"No, no, everything's fine. Andrew is well . . . we were just wondering here . . . are you planning your usual visit this Saturday?"

"Why, yes . . . yes, I am."

"I understand. Well . . . perhaps Mrs. Wakeham hasn't had an opportunity to speak to you."

"Speak to me about what, Mrs. Teale?"

"About tomorrow afternoon. She's coming for Andrew tomorrow afternoon."

"Coming for him?"

"Why, yes . . . to take him home for the holidays . . ."

"Oh, yes . . . of course, excuse me."

"We thought you might like to see him before then, Mr. Wakeham . . . unless, of course . . . well, perhaps you'll be seeing him over the holidays anyway . . ."

The poor woman is embarrassed. She must wish a thousand times a day that people like Molly and me could learn to manage our lives better.

"Mrs. Teale, it's good of you to call about this."

"It's no trouble, Mr. Wakeham."

I can hear the laughter of small children.

"Well, yes. I'd like to see Andrew before his mother comes for him tomorrow afternoon."

"I thought you would."

"Perhaps I could come tomorrow morning. Is that all right?"

"Well, it is irregular. We generally don't permit parents or visitors in the mornings. That's when the children are having their treatment sessions and their group games. But . . . these are unusual circumstances and it *is* Christmas. Yes, I think tomorrow morning about eleven will be fine."

"Very good, Mrs. Teale."

"I know Andrew looks forward to your visits."

"I enjoy seeing him, too."

"I know you do . . . I know you do . . . and we'll look forward to seeing *you* tomorrow at about eleven."

"Right, and thanks so much for calling, Mrs. Teale."

"It's no trouble, Mr. Wakeham, and Merry Christmas."

"Yes. Merry Christmas to you, too."

Mrs. Teale likes talking to me about house plants. They are her chief interest in life and she has a fine green thumb. She thinks I am a good fellow because I always stop to chat with her in one of the sunrooms when I visit Andrew.

We always take up our positions near one of the large bay windows which look across to the ravine and the back lawns of the Rosedale houses. I place a foot along the low bank of radiators and lean forward, resting an elbow on my knee. Mrs. Teale stands a little aback with her chunky arms folded across her chest like a farm woman. This way we can both admire the boxes of African violets and geraniums on the wide sills. Sometimes I will deliver a word of cautious praise or suggest a new nitrogen compound for quick growth. My greenhouse experience makes me more knowledgeable than most in these matters.

Mrs. Teale likes me better than Molly, who never takes time to stop and talk. She's also more sympathetic towards me and believes I'm more vulnerable. She's wrong, of course, but you could never convince her otherwise. Last Christmas I sent her a poinsettia. She still talks about it.

7.

The winter solstice is upon us in this northern hemisphere and through the window of Sydney Calhoun's office I can watch the afternoon's failing light. Sydney phoned me a few moments ago and asked me to come in for a little talk. We are seated by the window, bathed in a stark fluorescent glare like strangers in an evening railway coach. We are talking about our cars. In his antic way Sydney has spun his chair around and now straddles it, like a young doctor about to level with his patient. In this position his thighs look heavy as boles and his pants ride up his legs around muscular calves, exposing his gartered diamond socks. He is telling me about his Olds and its performance under winter driving conditions. In the darkening window I can see the reflection of Sydney's back. He is putting on weight these days and is quickly outgrowing his suit coats. This one is stretched so tightly across his shoulder blades that it looks ready to fly apart at the seams. Sydney is built like one of those Irish-American middleweights who used to turn up on the *Gillette Cavalcade of Sports* on Friday nights. He's a slope-shouldered man with a pleasant pie-shaped face. His powerful body looks as though it had been formed from some malleable substance like children's Plasticine. All the angles and edges of his frame have been softened and flexed so that he appears to have no bones beneath his flesh. Sydney is beginning to grow slack around the middle too, though he works out twice a week at the Y.M.C.A.

"So how long have you been with us now, Wes? Four months, isn't it?"

"Just about, Syd, yes . . ."

"And how are you liking it?"

"I'm really enjoying the work."

Sydney rests his forearms along the top of the chair and laces his broad fingers together. He opens his mouth in a half-yawn and a gold-filling gleams like a sunstone.

"Wes? I've been in this business now for twenty-three years and I've loved every minute of it. You've got to . . . I don't know how a man can go through his day if he doesn't enjoy his work . . . you know . . . before I got into school publishing I was on the road two years for General Biscuit and you can take it from me . . . there's a world of difference between talking to some corner grocer with Grade Seven and a man who has spent four years at a university studying European civilization . . ."

It is possible to sit here and talk to Sydney and not think of anything much. To nod my head and blink and look interested in what the man has to say. It's the least one can do. Yet sitting here listening to Sydney is making me as jumpy as an alcoholic. I have the greatest urge to spring up and pad about the room like a quick nervous cat.

". . . and you will have personality clashes with some people . . . you can't expect everybody to like you . . . that's unreasonable . . ."

Sydney is a *Digest* reader and a Lion. On Saturday mornings in winter you will find him driving the boys to the Community Centre for pee-wee hockey. He never misses the annual Father-and-Son Banquet in Lion Hall. Nor is he too proud to canvass door to door for United Appeal when the call for volunteers goes out. He even sings in the choir at the church of his choice. He is taking life by the throat and giving it a good shake. But sitting here listening to this solid roast-beef citizen makes me want to vault through that window and run down Britannia Road. A long muscle in the back of my neck is leaping like a spastic. Sydney is talking about the big sale to Universal Electronics Corporation.

". . . and it's difficult to say where it could lead . . . in the final analysis it will probably . . ."

I have mislaid some time here. It is impossible to say how much, five minutes . . . half an hour. I left my wrist watch on my desk by the porcelain ball. But it so happens that I am now leaning against Sydney's doorjamb with my hands clasped in front of me. Our talk must nearly be over and I must be on my way out. The thumb of my left hand is searching out the pulse along my right wrist. Sydney and I talk about the need to increase promotion efforts on the Primary Math Kit. I promise to try my hand at some copy. My heartbeat is truly alarming. Sydney waves good-bye and asks to be remembered to Bert and Mildred and Molly. I walk back towards my office, convinced I will have a thrombosis before I get there. These things happen. North American males are now having heart attacks in their early thirties. Only the other day in the dentist's office did I read this, my auricles and ventricles a-tremble. An article for the young executive's wife. Mrs. Bruner is neatly fitting the grey dust cover around her Smith Corona. Her eyes avoid me.

I am not seated one minute, however, before she knocks on my door and enters, standing cold of eye and unsmiling.

"I want to know, Mr. Wakeham. Is anything the matter?"

Her voice is as edgy as iron filings. Something is roiling around inside her. Clearly she's upset and looking for combat.

"What do you mean, Mrs. Bruner? I don't understand."

"You seem to be displeased with me today for some reason."

"Displeased? Why, no . . ."

"I suggest, Mr. Wakeham, that if you are unhappy with my work . . ."

"I'm not unhappy with your work, Mrs. Bruner . . ."

". . . we can both see Mr. Calhoun and . . ."

The Germans are a frank, earnest people. I do not want to quarrel with this frank, earnest German.

"I assure you, Mrs. Bruner, as far as I'm concerned your work is fine . . . excellent, in fact. It's just . . . I'm a little distracted today . . . I'm sorry."

"It's all right, Mr. Wakeham . . . I just wanted to be sure there was nothing wrong."

"No, no, nothing is wrong."

"Fine. I thank you. I will say good-night now."

"Yes, yes, good-night, Mrs. Bruner. Good-night."

Mrs. Bruner slides long smooth legs through the doorway. Home to Helmut with another tale.

A few days ago in the office mail there was a colourful brochure from Air Canada. I have it here before me. They want me to fly away to green islands and lie on some jewel of a beach by a tropical sea. Why not cut loose, they ask. In one corner of this brochure is a small perforated coupon which I am invited to send to them. The coupon says: *Dear Sky Pals: Yes, I want to cut loose. Please send me more information on Caribbean fun spots.* Caribbean fun spots? I am pretty certain that is not the answer, but I read on anyway, glancing up from time to time to watch the darkness fall across this winter afternoon, listening to my own wind escape, a long slow leak of sulphurous air that leaves me mildly nauseated.

8.

On Thursday evenings I watch *Run for Your Life* on one
of the Buffalo stations. The episodes are several years old
and I've seen this particular one before, but that's all right.
Old Ben is at it again. This time he is roaming around Paris
in the autumn, wearing a belted trench coat, drinking a
glass of wine in one of the deserted outdoor cafés and standing on the banks of the Seine to watch the leaves fall silently
into the dark solemn river. He looks so wistful and melancholy standing there brooding over his terminal disease
while he waits for the pretty young art student to show up
and fall in love with him. He looks wistful and melancholy
all right, but I do believe that deep inside, his heart is really
singing in its aliveness.

I watch old Ben and take a swig of aged Scotch from the Holocaust bottle. I am forced to note with dismay that there are not that many swigs left in the bottle. I shall be sorry to see it go. It is because of this bottle that Molly and I are now living under separate roofs. It is true. The Holocaust bottle was the cause of our last violent quarrel.

The quarrel arose out of the fact that one September afternoon while I was visiting schools Molly broke the ancient seal and poured a good healthy drink for herself and her old St. Helen's chum, Ernestine Hough. Now I am not a parsimonious man and normally I wouldn't have minded Molly drinking my whisky. But it so happens that she chose to drink from the Holocaust bottle and this put me in a fine rage.

This Holocaust bottle is a handsome round flagon of Chivas Regal which I bought at exactly twenty minutes past eleven o'clock on the morning of Wednesday, October 24, 1962. For many years now it has sat like an amber-glass Buddha in the cupboards and closets of my various dwellings. I am not particularly superstitious but I had come to regard this bottle of Scotch as something of a minor household god. Certainly I considered it every bit as inviolate as the Holy Ark and after five years of marriage Molly knew this. When I walked into the apartment that day and saw Molly and the Hough woman drinking from my Holocaust bottle, I fear I hurled abuse at the both of them. Molly finally threw a glass at me and told me to shove my goddam old bottle you know where. But they could have drunk gin or rye: there was plenty of that in the cupboard. For that matter, they could have walked across to the Shopping Plaza Liquor Store and bought a bottle of Scotch if Scotch was their fancy.

As I said, I bought the Holocaust bottle on the morning

of Wednesday, October 24, 1962, at exactly twenty minutes past eleven. I remember looking at the wall clock in the liquor store when the clerk handed me the brown paper bag. I wasn't missing much that morning. Although I kept no journal of that day's events, I can still recall details with peculiar vividness. The liquor-store clerk, for instance, was a thin fellow with large fan-like ears and a pencil moustache. He had a mole near his left nostril and in the pocket of his shirt was a package of Export cigarettes. In fact, I was feeling so sentient and aware on that cool and cloudy Wednesday, so consumed by the fires of my own aliveness, that at times I felt dizzy and faint with excitement. I know that at one point I stopped to lean against a mailbox. Someone had stuck a rolled newspaper through the slot and it still protruded several inches from the box. I can still remember the mailing address on the brown wrapping paper: Mr. Carl Hendrickson, 5498 Lolar Heights Drive, Calgary, Alberta. For several months after, I was to wonder from time to time what Mr. Hendrickson was doing on that particular morning.

From the liquor store I walked down Huron Street with the bottle of Chivas Regal under one arm and a copy of the *Toronto Daily Star* under the other. I had been living for several years in the Huron Street neighbourhood, moving from house to house whenever the cracks in the walls or the frayed edges of the rugs began to work their familiar gloomy spell. Most of the old dark brick homes along the street had been converted into rooming houses and rented to students. At this particular time, I was living at Mrs. Brown's. She was a fierce deaf old woman who quarreled with most of her tenants but seemed to like me. I have always gotten on with elderly women.

When I reached Mrs. Brown's that morning I stopped

in the hallway near her door to listen to the television news. I needn't have stopped, for Mrs. Brown's TV was always turned up full blast. In the evenings it was a constant source of irritation between the roomers and Mrs. Brown. No one on the same floor could hear himself think when she was watching television. In the daytime the noise was incredible. And now Walter Cronkite's confirmatory tones were pealing through the old deserted house, shaking the very timbers behind the plaster. As if in harmony with the grimness of the hour, my newspaper fell open to the terrible headlines: *25 Red Ships Steam On, Showdown Hours Away.* I listened for a few moments as Walter bore the grave tidings: *The Cabinet is still in emergency session . . . the President and the Secretary of State have conferred . . . Bobby Kennedy was not hopeful that . . .*

All these phrases were tearing loose and scattering through my mind like newspapers on a windy street. This may be the most important day in the history of the planet, I said to myself, and my lips were moving. The Russian ships were still steaming for Cuba and Mr. Kennedy had sworn to intercept them. Meanwhile, all those big firecrackers were sitting there waiting for the buttons to be depressed. After a couple of million years we had reached this point in time and I was standing in Mrs. Brown's hallway listening to Walter Cronkite. Through the oval window in the front door I watched a policeman fasten a yellow ticket to the windshield wiper of a grey Plymouth sedan of late-fifties vintage. Its licence number was 732092. Suddenly the door to Mrs. Brown's apartment opened and she was standing there looking up at me. Through the open door the sound of her TV rolled forward like a sonic boom and behind her I could see anxious grey faces flickering across the screen.

"Mr. Wakeham?" she cried. "What are you doing home?

Why aren't you at work this morning?" She was holding a bag of garbage in one hand and looking sharply at me, her watery blue eyes bright with excitement.

"Not feeling well today, Mrs. Brown," I shouted, "I'm going up to bed." I was used to her deafness and always shouted. It alarmed strangers to see us talking on the street, for they always assumed I was angry at the old lady when actually I was only trying to be understood.

"Aaargh," Mrs. Brown said in a strangled voice, "you're coming down with something. You look a little peaked. You young people don't know how to look after yourselves these days."

She jerked a claw-like hand towards her apartment. "Big doings, eh!"

"I'll say."

"It doesn't look so good right now," she said cheerfully.

"Is that so?"

"I don't think Kennedy'll break down and I, for one, hope he doesn't." She clamped her old tough jaws together. "Those Russians have got to be taught a lesson," she said.

"I suppose so," I replied glumly, one hand already on the banister.

"Aaargh," said Mrs. Brown again and stamped out the front door, hefting the bag of garbage in one hand.

In my room on the second floor I sat holding the bottle of Chivas Regal and listening to Mrs. Brown's TV. Even up there, it was coming in loud and clear. Earlier that morning I had phoned Steve Kandel, copy chief at Eckhardt, Baylor & Cohn, the advertising agency where I worked. I had told him that I thought I was coming down with something and had decided to stay home for the day. Steve was a breezy affable character, but the news was not welcome.

"Wes . . . you can't do this to me!" he cried hysterically.

"Listen now . . . Roper's mother-in-law or maybe his mother . . . Christ, I don't know . . . anyway she died last night and he's on a plane now to Winnipeg . . ."

Ben Roper was a fellow copywriter who was working with me on the Magic Mary Cake Mix account.

"I'm sorry, Steve, but I'm just not up to it. I have this temperature . . ."

"Sure, sure, you're faking, you bastard. That's malingering . . . goddamit, Wes, come on now. You know the deadline for this Magic Mary stuff is Friday. Have a heart, for Christ's sake."

"I know, Steve," I said. "I'll try to make it tomorrow, really . . ."

"Now, Wes, please," he pleaded. "Come in . . . look . . ." He was beginning to sound like the movie actor Rod Steiger, whom he slightly resembles.

"Ten one-minute spots. What is that to you, you little genius . . . I'll call in Harley to help. We'll have lunch, the three of us. I'm buying . . ."

"But I'm sick, Steve," I said earnestly. "I have this temperature. Maybe by tomorrow if I stay in bed . . ."

"Oh, Jesus H. Christ," he shouted and slammed the phone in my ringing ear.

Outside my bedroom window the black squirrel ran along the bare grey limbs of the elm and disappeared down his hole. For weeks now I had been watching him gather his winter stores—looking this way and that with his quick bright eye, running along the yellow grass by the house and up the scabrous old tree, his big tail twitching nervously at every sound. Now he poked his head through the hole again and sniffed the air for danger. I watched him for five minutes and then phoned Karen Schulyer.

Karen also worked at Eckhardt, Baylor & Cohn, as secretary to the manager of the Traffic Department. She was a tall, smooth-skinned girl with shapely legs and remarkable silver-blond hair which she always wore in a shortened page-boy style. This hair fit her head like a platinum helmet and gave her a rather grave bearing. Her eyes were ice blue and she had large front teeth that were slightly bucked. Instead of detracting from her looks, however, these teeth only tended to make her mouth wider and more sensuous, softening some of the boreal chill that seemed to surround her crisp Nordic handsomeness.

We had been seeing a lot of each other for several months and in her cool serious way Karen had me thinking hard about nuptials. Frankly she had much to offer as a life-long partner. Her mind was lively and interesting and she certainly looked good on one's arm at a visit to the theatre. Karen's only fault was her somewhat humourless grapple with life. She was one of those self-educated persons who leave high school at an early age and then a few years later discover that they have a tremendous curiosity about everything under the sun. This makes them feel unfulfilled and they are forever attending extension classes or signing up for the Great Books course. Karen was like that. As a matter of fact, she was taking anthropology lectures at the University that fall of sixty-two. I used to pick her up on Monday nights in front of the Engineering Building and bring her back to Mrs. Brown's. There we would lie on the bed while she talked about the sacrificial rites of New Guinea headhunters and I caressed her precious loving parts.

After a while she would get up and pad to the bathroom in her stockinged feet, her beige handbag slung over a shoulder. There she would flush the toilet and run tap water into the sink while she lifted a lovely ivory leg to the edge of the bathtub and inserted her diaphragm with a devilish-looking plastic prong, replacing the cap on the tube of vaginal cream and then washing and drying her hands as carefully as a surgeon. How do I know all this, you ask. One night I sneaked across from the bed and watched her through the keyhole.

After these stringent birth-control measures, Karen would appear by the bed with one of my terrycloth towels wrapped around her middle, looking like nothing so much as a beautiful captive Viking queen. In spite of her curiosity about things, though, Karen wasn't much for high jinks in bed and she once grew sulky when I suggested we try something different, using one of Mrs. Brown's slat-backed rocking chairs. In the conventional positions, however, you couldn't fault the girl.

Karen Schulyer had me nearly convinced that a life in advertising would be an acceptable way to pass the time. Certainly, I found it easy to write simple words which extolled the merits of various consumer products. Some of you may in fact remember the Magic Mary Cake Mix jingles which, in spite of Steve Kandel's anxiety, did get on the air.

> *Mary Mary, Magic Mary,*
> *What makes your cake mix the best?*
> *Why, sugar and spice and everythin' nice,*
> *And eggs that are fresh from the nest!*

I wrote that! It wasn't hard and moreover I was paid an excellent salary to do so. Karen was right about many things. The advertising life was not so bad and I could see a little future there with all those jingles in my head and the platinum-helmeted Karen by my side. We even talked about having two small well-behaved children to send to private school. After sexual intercourse Karen would often lie there in my arms and think about our future. Sometimes she would disclose her plans, asking me if I minded her dreaming like that. I didn't mind. She had calculated that if we both worked for three years and were careful with our money we could probably put away enough for a down payment on some viney Tudor cottage in one of the leafier parts of town. It sounded good to me. Even Karen's intense efforts at self-improvement began to affect me. I sallied out one day and paid several hundred dollars for a telescope to study the heavens. I joined a science-book club and bought a giant anthology of poetry for the bedside table. Although she was irritated by my extravagance with the telescope, Karen was pleased that I was taking up astronomy. It seemed to her like a fine hobby for an advertising man.

And so I would fill my allotted time on this planet with a few harmless diversions—plan me a little future with the jingles in my head and my platinum-helmeted partner by my side. With my Tudor cottage on the leafy street and my two small well-behaved children in the private school. Although I was not completely sold on this course, that roughly was my state of mind during the late summer and fall of 1962 when, on a grey Wednesday, the twenty-fourth day of the tenth month, at ten minutes past ten, Eastern Standard Time, I stopped looking at the black squirrel and picked up the phone to call Karen Schulyer.

The line was busy and it took me several minutes to reach her. Finally, though, her crisp voice was crackling through the wires.

"Wes, what are you doing home?" she asked suspiciously. "I just saw Steve Kandel a few moments ago. Ben Roper's away too, and Steve looks simply furious."

"He's worried about the Magic Mary campaign," I said.

"Well, aren't you?" she asked, amazed. "It's one of your accounts, isn't it?"

"Karen? . . . Have you read the morning paper or listened to the radio?"

"Oh, this Cuba thing," she said quietly. "Yes, isn't it awful? Everyone here is talking about it." She paused. "What's the matter with *you*, anyway? You looked fine last night. Are you sick?"

"Yes."

"Oh, honey, I'm sorry. What is it?"

"Karen, I want you to come over and see me. Come over for lunch. I'll get a bottle of wine."

"Say, are you really sick?" She laughed. "What are you up to, anyway?"

"Please, Karen. Take the afternoon off and come over."

"I can't do that, Wes."

"Tell them you've got your monthlies or something."

"Wes, now really," she whispered crossly.

"Listen, Karen, I don't like the looks of this damn Cuban thing."

"Oh, is that it?" She laughed again. "Oh, Wes, I'm sure they'll work something out."

"How can you be so sure?"

"Look! Aren't you a little over-excited about all this?"

"Over-excited," I cried. "Yes, I suppose I am. But I don't like all those fucking bombs and missiles that both sides have in their corners."

"Listen here now." I am sure she must have stamped her foot under the desk. "You don't have to start using that kind of language. And if you're not sick I'd advise you to get down here. Kandel is really mad."

"Oh, screw Kandel."

"Wes, you shouldn't talk like that. The man's only trying to do his job."

"Yes, yes . . ."

"I really think you ought to come down now. Look, I have to go. Old Jason's due any minute. Let's have lunch. I was supposed to eat with Janey, but I'll cancel. Okay?"

"I'm not going down there, Karen," I said, peevish as a sick child. "I want you to come up here. I'll get a bottle of wine. I'll make an omelette . . ."

"Wes," she said fiercely, "I'm not going up there and that's final. Now you're just being silly about this whole thing."

"Well, maybe I am, and then maybe I'm not, goddamit," I announced grandly and hung up. I arose trembling and walked to the window. The black squirrel was making another trip down the tree trunk to the damp yellow grass. Mrs. Brown's TV was still blaring away, only now it was transmitting a serial drama. Perhaps the situation is not so bleak afer all, I thought. Someone's unmarried daughter was pregnant. What splendid news! Bits and pieces of the dialogue are still floating around in my head, like wreckage from a stricken vessel.

WOMAN'S VOICE (*cold as marble*): This is going to kill your father, Betty.

BETTY'S VOICE (*broken and weeping*): Oh, Mummy! Don't say that, please.

MUMMY'S VOICE (*colder still*): Well, it will. I just know it will.

Oh, Betty! Oh, Mummy! I repeated to myself and my lips were moving as if in prayer. A thousand thanks for your small miseries! Oh, hack writers and gimcrack directors! Please keep churning out your squalid little stories. Only keep that other big show off the air! Keep Walter's sad American face from Mrs. Brown's living-room screen!

Then my telephone rang and it was Karen. She was furious.

"Wes Wakeham," she said, "don't you ever hang up in my face again."

"Karen . . . I . . ."

"Don't you ever . . . ever . . . do that again."

"Karen, please . . . will you come over and see me . . ."

"I am *not* going over there, goddamit," she hissed, and for the second time that day someone slammed a phone in my ringing ear.

Oddly enough, those were the last words Karen and I ever spoke to one another. In the office the next day I found my smooth-skinned Viking deep in a polar sulk. I was used to these silences and I generally gave her three or four days and then thawed her out with an invitation to lunch. This time, however, I didn't bother, for it had come to me on that October Wednesday that I wasn't really much interested in a little future with the platinum-helmeted Karen. And I was forced to reflect that even if I were interested I could never really bring myself to believe that such things would ever come to pass.

A couple of weeks later, I walked into Steve Kandel's office and told him I was finished with the jingles too. When I walked out the door of Eckhardt, Baylor & Cohn for the last time, I passed within a few feet of Karen Schulyer's desk. She was typing away and she never looked up. As a matter of fact, I never saw the girl again.

After Karen Schulyer slammed the phone in my ringing ear that Wednesday morning I sat for a good long time, staring out the window at the elm tree and waiting for the black squirrel to return. This homely vigil seemed to calm me. It was then that I walked out and bought my fine fat flagon of Chivas Regal—the Holocaust bottle.

1 1 8.

When I returned to my room I sat in the slat-backed rocking chair and listened to Mrs. Brown's TV. The twelve o'clock news was not good; into Walter's voice had crept an edgy note. I had not noticed this before and it was as vaguely disquieting as seeing one's father flinch with pain. Mr. Kennedy was standing firm and the word from the Russians was not reassuring. They wanted the Americans to scrap their bases in Turkey. You are a bunch of hypocrites, Mr. Khrushchev was reported to have said.

Shortly before one o'clock my palms began to sweat and I picked up the telephone and called a tall willowy young woman named Molly Sinclair. I had met her at a fraternity party a few weeks before. Fraternity parties were never much a part of my recreation, but on that particular Friday night Karen was off to a bridal shower and a college friend named Joel Brewer phoned and invited me to this party. Molly was a big smiling brown-haired chunk of a girl, strapping as a lioness and smelling of lemon soap. I stood talking to her for hours, smiling until my cheeks ached. We got on well, I think. We talked about Robert Browning. In the afternoon she had listened to a lecture on the poet and she was still excited by the professor's remarks. We sat finally in a dark room upstairs with a bottle of London Dry gin between us and we listened to the shouting and the absurd football songs ringing through the old house. And we chattered merrily on about Fra Lippo Lippi and the old Duchess. Now and then I would steal a blithe kiss and once or twice I placed a hand beneath her cashmere sweater and felt a warm beating breast. Later in the evening she gave me the telephone number of her sorority house. And now on this October Wednesday I called that house, half-persuaded that she would never be home at this hour of the day. As it turned out, she answered the phone.

1 1 9.

"Hello," she said in that cool throaty voice.

"Hello," I replied as gawky as a schoolboy. "Um . . . I wonder . . . would that be Molly Sinclair by any chance?"

"Why, yes."

"This is Wes Wakeham, Molly."

"Who?"

"Wes—"

"Oh, the Browning man."

"That's right."

"How are you?" She sounded amused.

"Fine, thanks." I was the Brylcreemed boy in the phone booth. "Look, I was wondering . . . I know it's awfully short notice, but would you happen to be free this afternoon?"

She laughed. "Why, whatever for, Mr. Browning?" she asked, as coy as a Southern belle.

"Ha, ha . . . well, I was wondering whether perhaps you mightn't like to have a few drinks . . . with me."

She laughed a rich deep laugh. "Well, it's a little early in the day, isn't it?"

"I suppose it is," I said desperately, "but . . ."

"Don't you work?"

"Oh, yes," I replied quickly, "but I've got the day off. It seemed like a good idea to have a few drinks with a beautiful girl and . . ."

"Ho, ho. That's a bit rich, Browning . . ."

I laughed idiotically. "Yes, it is, isn't it."

The next thing I would be scuffing my shoes and saying Aw shucks.

"Look . . . can I come over and see you?"

"Well now, I'd really like that," she said, "and it sounds just marvellously decadent to be drinking this early in the day . . . but I've got this psych lecture at two-thirty and I really can't afford to miss it . . ."

I snorted like the village simpleton. "Couldn't I perhaps persuade you to cancel the psych lecture? I mean just for today . . ."

"I really don't think so." She was matter-of-fact as a secretary. "I missed the last one, and you know . . . these things can catch up on you after a while . . ."

"Well, yes . . . yes, they can . . ." I was faltering.

"But I'm free Friday night," she added.

"Yes," I replied. "Well, fine. Maybe we could see each other then."

"Yes, I'd really like that, Browning."

"That's fine," I mumbled. "I'll pick you up around eight o'clock . . ."

"Wonderful . . . what shall I wear?"

"Wear?" I repeated numbly. "Oh, anything at all . . ."

"Oh, really, and where are we going?"

"I don't know yet," I said helplessly. "Maybe we'll take in a Browning lecture . . ."

She laughed, delighted with me. "Why you're really an amusing fellow, Browning," she said.

"Yes, I am," I said, hanging up the phone with great care.

There was nothing to do then but sit in the slat-backed rocking chair and wait. I would sit there in my little cell like a monk of old, watchful of everything in my aliveness, my five senses thrumming like plucked strings. But unlike a monk of old I would not tell my beads or pray to the Heavenly Father. It had been clear for some time now that the Heavenly Father had taken off and was now living among the stars of another galaxy. And so I sat there, as every bit alive as Adam on the first morning, listening to the news with a cocked ear, clutching the Holocaust bottle.

Mrs. Brown switched channels again. A man was cooking

an omelette. His voice was flat, out of the Middle West. He could have been a used-car salesman from some place like Gary, Indiana. *Now listen, girls . . . There are only two ways to cook an omelette . . . the wrong way . . . and my way* [laughter] *. . . So look now* [chuckles] *. . . you start with an egg . . . right?* [chuckles] *. . . One of these* [laughter followed by mild applause].

It occurs to me as I listen to the omelette man that I am living through the greatest diversion of them all. This is what makes me tingle with aliveness. This is what puts the quick bright eye in Mrs. Brown's head and makes her dart about like the black squirrel. All the emptiness and sadness of our days has been blown away by the great black wind which now sweeps across the sky. It scours the air and leaves it bitter and sharp as ammonia. Everything has meaning and nothing can be ignored. We are fearfully alive—Mrs. Brown and I.

I sit in the room and listen to the omelette man and think about my father. Over twenty years have passed since he left his flour mill in search of this feeling. But he had his nights of laughing girls and the tavern songs (All right now! All together, lads! Rooooooll out the barrrrel . . . we'll have a bar-rel o' fun). He had his voyage across the dark enchanted ocean and his Sunday walks in the country churchyards that smelled of lilacs and earth. He had his damn rooks high above the cornfields and his bugle calls on the battlegrounds.

Mrs. Brown had switched channels yet again. Someone was now interviewing a senator from one of the Western states, Nevada or Montana. I lay down on the bed as rigid as a stick and stared at the ceiling. The senator allowed that the situation looked serious, but he was confident that reason would prevail. I thought of taking a nip from the

Holocaust bottle but decided against it. Instead, I removed my trousers and undershorts and masturbated. Mrs. Brown was back with the cooking school. I fell asleep to a Jello commercial and didn't awaken for thirteen hours.

So ended my October Wednesday of 1962. Of course the great black wind blew itself out eventually and Mrs. Brown and I were able to sink back again into our gloom. The Holocaust bottle, however, has remained with me—companion to my wanderings, pristine and magical, emitting a little presence all its own in the cupboards and closets of my various dwellings. That is, until the day this September past when Molly and Ernestine Hough broke the seal and had a drink.

Now it is nearly finished. I will take another swig and toast old Ben. He has just bidden farewell to the young art student and climbed into a taxi for the airport. He has left her sitting there in the deserted café—a lovely little piece, as round and ripe as an autumn apple.

9.

I am a good listener and I can dip my head to one side and smile when people tell me about their jobs and dealings. George Gruber is a bashful, pleasant young man—about my own age with mild blue eyes and a blond brush-cut. He teaches mathematics to grades nine and ten at Union Place Secondary School. We are standing—George and I—in one corner of Harold Pendle's living room and talking about the price of suburban real estate. George bought his house five years ago and he figures it is already worth six thousand more on the current market. In another twenty years, he says, the price could triple. It sounds like a shrewd investment to me and I tell him as much. This makes him so happy that he touches me lightly on the arm and asks me to come around and see him at the school in the new year. During our talk he keeps throwing anxious glances across the room at his wife, a plump little redhead with a pretty face. She is laughing and talking to a giant of a man whose high dome brow glistens in the light. He towers over everyone in the room and he has to bend forward to hear. This he does with great charm, smiling down at George's wife, with his hands clasped behind his back like a clergyman. George has told me that his name is Ted Garowski and he's head of the Mathematics Department at Union Place Secondary.

As our conversation begins to dry up, George commences to snap the fingers of one hand along his trouser leg and hums to the music on Harold's phonograph, the Broadway show *Cabaret*. In the little group next to us a nervous dark-haired girl is also keeping time with the catchy music. She is moving her head from side to side as if she would like to be asked to dance. She smiles and nods as a small middle-aged man describes his most unruly student. As he talks to the girl, the little man makes a continual nervous adjustment to his granny glasses, using his right forefinger to push them back over the high ridge of his nose.

George Gruber and I look around the room and smile and clear our throats. We would both like to refill our punch glasses, but we are both embarrassed at having drained them so quickly. To cover up our embarrassment, we invent a little game of metaphors. George says with a shy grin that it's time to take on more fuel, while I hold up my empty glass and allow that we can't possibly fly on one wing. To tell the truth, we are both growing tired of one another. George would like to get back to his wife and I would prefer to move out of this corner. As it develops, the host himself rescues us from each other. Harold makes his way across the crowded room towards us, stopping now and then to chat with a little knot of people, stroking his thin pale cheeks, looking natty and collegiate in his Black Watch sports jacket and cuffless grey slacks. Harold nods to George and draws me aside, gripping my elbow like a policeman.

"Have you got a minute?"

"Sure thing."

"I'd like to show you something."

"Fine."

Still holding my elbow, Harold steers me across the room and through the hallway to the kitchen. There we pass around a table loaded with cups and saucers and platters of sandwiches and cookies. Harold opens a door and we silently descend a stairway to a large bright basement. It is a clean open place, painted a sensible ship's grey and smelling faintly of laundry and wood shavings. Along one wall is Harold's workbench, a polished yellow slab of maple. It looks as sturdy and redoubtable as a monastery door. As I pass by, I experience the greatest urge to rap the bench smartly and feel its worth. At one end is a gleaming steel vise holding in its jaws a piece of bevelled wood—part of an unfinished window sill. The wall behind is covered with hand and power tools hanging from large hooks and nails. I feel a twinge of envy for Harold and his orderly world. I used to dream of evenings by such a bench as this, making little things from shapeless hunks of sweet-smelling wood, watching the bookcases and birdhouses grow beneath my hands, gaining the homely solid comfort of awl and hammer.

Above us the dull drone of the party works its way through the floorboards and joists. Some of the people are dancing and the heavy drag of their shoes scrapes the air over our heads. I turn to Harold, who is selecting a key from a silver chain.

"I didn't know you were a handyman, Harold."

"Yes. I like to putter. Nothing too complicated, mind you."

"This still looks tricky to me."

"Oh, that's for a new window I'm putting in the garage. There's nothing to it, really."

But Harold is being modest. There looks to be a great deal to it and he is probably a painstaking craftsman. He stoops now to unlock a door and I follow him through to a small windowless room, blinking at the light.

"Welcome to the sanctum sanctorum," Harold says, closing the door behind me. "This is my retreat from the world. Not even Edna gets in. Except to dust, of course."

From somewhere a fan begins to churn the warm stale air. The little room is mysterious and exudes a mildly sinister atmosphere. In such a room as this, prisoners have been questioned for hours by men with black truncheons. It contains only a plywood desk and swivel chair and along one side a row of several metal lockers of the sort one sees in high-school corridors. On the wall in front of the desk is a large oil painting of a seascape. Heavy green surf breaks across a deserted shore, the waves curling into white foam as they crest. The sky is dark and lowering with a solitary seagull drifting down on the wind. The picture is not well executed and in this little dungeon-like room it looks out of place and oddly silly. Harold catches me staring at it.

"Edna painted it," he says looking up with me. "Three years ago. We took a holiday on the Gaspé coast of Quebec."

"Is that so?"

"We call it 'The Lonely Grandeur of the Sea.' It reminds me of Tennyson's poem . . ."

"Oh, yes?"

"You know the one. Break, break, break, on thy cold grey stones, O sea!"

"Oh, yes. Yes, I do . . ."

There is a pause and the hum of the fan seems to fill the room with tinny noise.

"Well now," Harold says finally, and drops into the swivel chair as though he's been felled by a gunshot. He folds his hands across his stomach and stretches out his long thin legs, looking like a man trying hard to relax. But slumped in the swivel chair like this, he only appears embarrassed and uncomfortable and I find myself wishing that he would sit bolt upright as he used to do in the classrooms of old Middlesburgh High. I realize now that he wants to talk about his grammar book. He would probably like to know what the people at Winchester House think. I made a silent oath to speak to Sydney about this at the first opportunity and frame an evasive answer in my mind.

Now Harold leans forward and drops his hands onto the desk. The swivel chair creaks beneath him.

"The book is coming along well, Wakeham, and I've really got you to thank for it."

"Oh, now, I wouldn't exactly say that . . ."

"Yes, it's true. Your suggestion of sample chapters and outline was just what I needed to get me going."

He looks up at me and raises sand-coloured eyebrows.

"Do you know I've roughed out two more chapters since I sent that material to you?"

"Why, that's fine, Harold . . ."

"Here . . . let me show you."

He stands up, unfolding his long frame. In two strides he reaches one of the wall lockers and stoops down. Through the partly opened door of the locker I can see, of all things, several cans of Heinz pork and beans. He returns to the chair and places a large black pebbled binder on the desk. I lean forward like a man about to be shown a photograph album, one hand touching the back of Harold's chair and the other settled on the desk. The weight of my body bleaches the knuckles on the desk hand a sickly white and I find myself staring grimly at the abscence of blood around the bones. The handwriting in Harold's binder is precise and neat as a captain's log. *For years, standard grammar texts have forbidden the use of like as a conjugation. Most persons today, however, recognize . . .*

"This is my chapter on connectives," Harold says, tapping the page with a finger. "I've adopted a fairly flexible approach. A lot of the teachers aren't going to like it, particularly the older ones."

"No, I would guess not."

Harold seizes a ruler and runs the metal edge along the palm of his hand. It leaves a shallow pink trench in the flesh.

"But, heaven's sake, you can't teach old-line grammar to today's kids. They just don't listen to you. They hear things on television, you know. It's pointless and self-defeating to ignore the influence of these new media."

"That's true. I was reading only the other day . . ."

"Wakeham? . . . I'd like to send these two additional chapters along to your people. I'll have them finished over the holidays. What do you think?"

"Well, yes, that sounds fine, Harold. I guess you've been wondering why you haven't heard more definite news. The fact is that these decisions take time and . . ." Harold takes the ruler and saws away at one finger.

"Oh, I realize all that. It's not worrying me. We're making progress here all the time, that's the main thing. I think your people are entitled to take plenty of time to reach a decision . . ." He gazes up at The Lonely Grandeur of the Sea and frowns slightly, balancing the ruler now on an out-stretched finger. It wavers for a second and then corrects itself, lying there in perfect equilibrium. I straighten up and flex my fingers to restore circulation.

"I've been wondering, though. You don't suppose that sending these two chapters along will give your editors the idea that I'm pressing them for a decision."

"Not at all. As a matter of fact, I think it's a good idea. It's bound to give them a better notion of the shape and structure of the book."

"Do you really think so?"

"Absolutely . . . yes."

The ruler slides off his finger and falls to the desk with a clatter. He gazes upward once more at The Lonely Gran-deur of the Sea and then asks a question that never fails to amuse me, though I'm always careful not to smile.

"What do you want out of life, Wakeham?" he asks. "What's your goal?"

"I'm not sure, Harold, but . . ."   .

"You know . . . a man can slide along from day to day doing his job, raising a family, visiting friends, and it's all very fine. There's certainly satisfaction in that. But I've discovered that until a man reaches out for something, he never really experiences fulfillment in any meaningful sense of that word."

"Not many realize this."

"You are *so* right there."

He leans back in the swivel chair, resting his elbows along the arms, the long fingers describing a perfect Gothic arch.

"Would you like to see roughly five years' work?"

"Well . . ."

"Just a moment."

He unfolds himself once again and goes to the lockers. There he opens a door and steps aside, like a man inviting one to enjoy the view through his window. The bottom of the locker is piled high with black pebbled binders, but it is the tins of Dole Sliced Pineapple that attract my eye. The shelf near the top of the locker is filled with them.

"Those notes represent five years of weekends and summer vacations," Harold says, looking down at the binders. I can only purse my lips and send forth a low soft whistle of amazement, a gesture which pleases Harold very much. He smiles and snaps the locker door shut. The metallic twang echoes off the walls and makes me jump in my shoes. Harold shakes his head.

"I just hope your people realize that this project is not something I've entered into lightly."

"I'm sure they will."

"And you really think it's a good idea to show them these two new chapters?"

"Yes, I do."

"I see . . . Well, I'm going to shoot them along, then, in three weeks."

"Fine. We'll look forward to getting them."

Harold moves towards the door and stops.

"Oh, incidentally, there is one thing I wanted to mention. You'll probably find yourself talking to Duncan MacCauley upstairs. He's head of our department. I'd appreciate it if you didn't mention *Reflexive Grammar* at all."

"All right. Mum's the word."

"Good."

Harold seems to relax a little now. Standing by the door, he works his shoulders around inside the snappy sports jacket.

1 3 1.

"What do you think of my little sanctum sanctorum?" he asks.

"Well now, it looks very nice. Quiet and cozy. I would guess it's a dandy place to work."

"Excellent."

He abruptly strikes the wall with the flat of his hand. "That's all soundproofed. It's called Franklin board. An engineering friend of mine told me about it."

"Is that so?"

Harold and I stand back a little to regard the walls of his sanctum sanctorum. Actually, Harold is selling me the walls, pointing out the features of the Franklin board, stooping down now to run his fingers along the trim, his Masonic ring flashing across the wall like a cold bright eye. I bend down beside him and we both crouch there, rocking a little on our heels. Behind the door is a small stack of books, and by turning my head just so, I can read the titles along the spines: *The Holy Bible, The Globe Shakespeare, A Family Treasury of Good Stories, Everyman's Medical Guide.* As we straighten up to leave, it strikes me that I am standing in Harold Pendle's bomb shelter. Out of curiosity I ask him if this is true. He looks grave and strokes his cheeks.

"Yes. I built it after the Cuban crisis in sixty-three."

"Ah . . . that would be sixty-two . . ."

"What?"

"The Cuban crisis was in sixty-two."

"Are you sure about that?"

"Yes, positive." He's not convinced but lets it go.

"Well, perhaps you're right. Anyway, I built it after that. We'd just moved in here and I felt we should have something in the event of a nuclear attack. I don't go along with those people who simply wring their hands and say nothing can be done. I know that if there is a direct hit, we're not likely to survive. But, on the other hand, if we're only on the periphery, I believe we can live quite comfortably down here for at least two weeks. Most people don't like to talk about this business. It depresses them. They don't want to face the cold hard facts."

"That's true."

"I'll bet you yourself never give it so much as a thought from one day to the next."

"Not much more, I'm afraid."

"There, you see."

Harold closes the door to his bomb shelter, rattling the doorknob like a night watchman. I stand by the workbench and listen to the music from *Cabaret*. The entire house seems to be vibrating with it.

"I appreciate your advice about these two new chapters," Harold says, turning towards me.

"That's all right, Harold. Glad to help."

He stops for a moment and searches my face with his ice-blue eyes. "You know, Wakeham, it's a shame we didn't know each other a little better in high school. I believe we have quite a lot in common."

"It is a shame, yes . . ."

"If you don't mind my saying so, though, I always found you just a little on the wishy-washy side in those days."

"Well, I was a little, I guess. Still am, really." I am grinning like an idiot, but Harold merely strokes his cheek again and frowns.

"You were never a Scout, were you?"

"No."

"Too bad."

In Harold's living room I stand near the edge of a group and listen to the weekenders talk. The man next to me has just bought a snowmobile and he has it carefully hidden away in his neighbour's garage. On Saturday night when everyone is asleep he and the neighbour are going to haul the snowmobile into his living room and put it near the tree. We all agree that it is an excellent plan and tell him that we wish we could be there on Christmas morning, to see the faces of his wife and children. Edna Pendle, tall and slender in a green dress, sways among us like a reed in the wind. She offers biscuits and cheese from a platter.

I chat with the snowmobile man and watch a girl in the next group. It happens to be the nervous dark-haired girl—the one who likes to move her head in time to the music. She has been casting furtive glances my way and I have the impression that she would like to be introduced. However, I may be entirely wrong about this.

The nervous dark-haired girl is in her late twenties. I think she is beginning to grow used to the idea of spinster-hood: it is written into her plain intelligent face. She is also starting to put on some middle-aged weight and most of it is settling in her lower trunk, broadening her hips and rear and thickening her legs, making her a little bottle-shaped. The upper part of her body, though, doubtless looks the same as it did ten years ago in high school, flat-chested and skinny-armed. For all this, she is not a bad-looking woman and there is even a certain sexiness to her, an emanation that flows from a body taken for granted and used sparingly. She reminds me a little of Rosemary, only older and somehow earthier. I would guess, though, that like Rosemary she isn't particularly worried about her armpits or fingernails.

She probably lives alone in one of the new high rises on Napier Avenue or over in Meadowbank Park. She buys a new compact every other year and drives it back and forth to Union Place Secondary School each day and to the Shopping Plaza on Saturday mornings. Once a month she aims it down the highway towards the small town where she was born. There she spends a despairing weekend with retired Dad and Mom, trying to read her novel, smiling at her brother's children, and taking a lot of good-natured kidding about boy friends from her silly sister-in-law. Like me, she probably watches a fair amount of television and once a month or so she goes to the movies.

She is not particularly looking forward to Christmas in the small town with Mom and Dad and the nephews and nieces. She is more likely to be looking forward to a few good late shows over the holidays, a movie or two, and the new novel from the library. She looks a little mixed up, this nervous dark-haired girl, a little unsure about anarchy and freedom, free enterprise and socialism, agnosticism and atheism, despotism and democracy. She can see everyone's viewpoint only too clearly and she is trying to figure it all out and still be fair. She looks to me to stand a better than even chance of cracking up before she reaches her middle thirties. Right now she looks as high-strung as a greyhound, standing there smoking a cigarette and hugging her bare arms as she listens to the handsome black man from Barbados. He is talking about poverty in his homeland, enunciating carefully in his soft, clipped accent.

"You see . . . thee prub-lum . . . dee-munds ay new ayproach."

The girl looks up into his dark intense face and nods gravely, trying hard to understand what it must be like to be poor and black in the West Indies.

Meanwhile, I have become disengaged somehow from the snowmobile group and am floating freely as an amoeba, waiting to link up with other wandering cells. I can see George Gruber standing near the piano. He has a good hold on his wife's plump freckled arm and seems to be enjoying himself now, talking to three or four other men and shaking his small head from time to time. I am thinking of a trip to the john when someone lays hold of my arm. The grip is like a clamp in the flesh.

"Looking over the stuff, my friend?"

It's the insane little chemistry teacher Bellamy, all scrubbed and grinning above a checked sports jacket and bow tie.

"How are you?" he says, sticking out a hand.

"Fine, thanks."

"It's Walt, isn't it?"

"No, Wes . . . Wes Wakeham."

"Oh, yes. How are you, Wes? Do you remember me? Hank Bellamy?"

"Sure . . . nice to see you, Hank."

Bellamy looks over the room and wiggles his neck inside the collar of his shirt, his hand moving up to press the bow tie into place. He looks like a man standing in the stag line at a public dance. Now he makes a quick washing motion with his muscular hands and turns towards me. I can smell alcohol on his breath.

"So what's going on anyway? I just arrived."

"Oh, not too much. It's a good party, though."

"Yeh . . . these Christmas parties. They're all the same, a friggin' pain in the ass. . . . You a friend of Pendle's?"

"Well . . . we went to school together."

"You don't say? University?"

"No . . . high school."

"Uh, huh. Well, I am going to tell you something, my friend," he says, dropping his voice to a whisper. "The facts are these. Pendle wouldn't be caught dead in the same room with me if I weren't head of a department. As far as that

1 3 6.

goes, not many of these jokers would. I'm not exactly the most popular guy at Union Place Secondary School, you know. But I am head of a goddam department and the best friggin' chemistry man in Ontario and they all know it. . . . You heard of *Senior Chemistry for Today?*"

"Yes, of course . . . a standard text in the field."

"Right, and twelve years now on the department's list. Listen here, *Senior Chemistry for Today* by Schaeffer, Todd, Axelworth, and Bellamy. Only Bellamy did most of the work. In fact, Bellamy wrote the bloody book and they all know it. Everyone knows it."

Bellamy plunges his hands deep into his trouser pockets and looks out over the room once more.

"Just look at Pendle," he whispers, "trying to suck up to old Dunc MacCauley. What a friggin' fossil that Mac-Cauley is! You see, my boy, your friend Pendle there is angling for the assistant headship in his department. I would bet any money that's the reason for this friggin' party. MacCauley's going to name his man some time in the new year. I'd say your friend there has as good a chance as anyone."

Bellamy and I stand apart from the others with our hands in our pockets. I am watching Harold Pendle use his fine long fingers to illustrate a point to Duncan MacCauley, an older man in bifocals and grey gabardine. Bellamy is watching the black man and the nervous dark-haired girl. After a moment he nudges me with his elbow and whispers out of the side of his mouth like an old movie gangster.

"Helen better watch herself there or old Jeremy'll be in her pants before the night's over."

He hitches up his trousers and whispers again. "Have you ever seen one in the raw?"

"How's that?"

"A black boy. Have you ever seen one in the shower? We had one in our platoon in the service . . . a boy from Halifax. Name was Jimmy Howe, helluva nice guy. And, boy, was he hung? The friggin' thing fell halfway to his knees. . . . They're all the same, you know. Everyone of them's got enough for three white men. Once the girls get a taste of that, my friend, we don't stand a chance. Which reminds me. I heard a damn funny story the other day. As a matter of fact, another book salesman told me. There was this black boy, see . . . name's Rufus. And he's got this friggin' big tool. . . . Anyway, he can never get a pair of pants with crotch enough to fit him. So he goes to this little Jewish tailor . . ."

I listen to Bellamy's outrageous story and plan my departure. It is growing late and I have had enough of Harold Pendle's pre-holiday get-together. But suddenly the nervous dark-haired girl is making her way towards us. She arrives just as Bellamy delivers the punch line, collapsing into laughter and slapping his knee like a burlesque comic. Bellamy is right about the story. It *is* funny and I have to laugh. The girl smiles at us with her brown eyes.

"Hi, Hank. Another one of your famous stories?"

"Oh, Helen! I'd love to tell you but you're too young and pure of mind."

"Oh, sure."

"Do you know this young fellow, by the way? He's a travelling salesman and he's been around. He knows a story or two himself."

"Oh, really."

The girl gives me a cool ironic smile. I shrug innocently.

"My name's Wes Wakeham."

She offers a warm, moist hand. "Helen Corbett."

"What was old Jeremy bending your ear about, Helen?"

Bellamy asks. "Dee con-dishun of dee black pee-puples?"

"Now, Hank, really . . . Jeremy is all right. You shouldn't make fun of him like that."

"Can I get you something to drink?" I ask.

"Yes, *please*. I'd love another."

When I return, Helen Corbett is standing alone, still hugging her arms as though she were chilled. Bellamy has drifted into a group of older men which includes the dome-headed mathematics man. I hand the drink over. She smiles and looks out over the room.

"Thanks very much. You need quite a few of these to feel anything, it seems. In fact, I would say dear sweet Harold wasn't exactly lavish with the alcohol in his punch."

"Well," I laugh, "I was about to say the same thing to anyone who would listen. Actually, I could stand a good stiff double Scotch."

"Here, here."

Our conversation now gathers in upon itself and becomes a full-scale put down of Harold's party. Everything from Hank Bellamy's dirty jokes to Duncan MacCauley's gabardine trousers are raked with a mild pleasing scorn. Near the lighted Christmas tree we talk in whispers, like two bored teen-agers at a movie. Our remarks are unfair and ungracious and not terribly funny but they bring us together and we are soon hitting it off, feeling comfortable with one another in our isolation.

It is during the carol sing that I ask her to have a drink with me. At the piano Edna Pendle, her thin shoulder blades fluttering beneath the green dress like wings, is leading us through "Deck the Halls." Everyone, even Hank Bellamy, is in lusty voice. I move my lips but cannot crack a note. Beside me, Helen Corbett sings in a clear sweet alto. When I lean over to ask her, she merely nods her head and continues singing. I find this casual nod so enticing that during the third stanza of the carol, standing in the midst of these people with my hands in my pockets, it becomes necessary to give my organ a small rapturous squeeze.

Later, on the frozen street we stand—Helen Corbett and I—listening to "Hark the Herald Angels Sing" and watching the snow fall across the lights of Harold Pendle's sign which blinks forth Season's Greetings to one and all. Several of Harold's neighbours have decorated their houses with outdoor lights and it becomes easy to imagine that one is not standing in a suburban street at all but has in fact wandered up the lane of some northern Disneyland where Santa and his helpers actually dwell. I half-expect to see the pointed cap of an elf peeking around the corner of one of the houses.

Helen Corbett and I stand by the Dart and shake the new-fallen snow from our collars, trying to decide on a course. Helen looks more comely out of doors in her Doctor Zhivago costume. The fur-trimmed hood makes quite a fetching oval of her face, and the flaring military coat and high boots admirably suit her body. Standing here in the snowy street, she is altogether as handsome and secretive as a Russian officer's concubine. But something has gone seriously wrong and both of us appear to be suddenly wearied with one another. It demands a great effort to keep things going. The spark that jumped between us in Harold's living room is now sputtering fitfully and threatening to go out at any moment. Held together briefly by our cleverness and wisecracking, we now find ourselves cast on these lonely shores—two tired strangers trying to be polite to one another. In fact, I do believe that if one of us were to suggest that it might not be such a bad idea to forget about the drink, bid each other farewell and make our separate retreats into the night, the other would not mind at all. The whole business leaves me saddened and I would like nothing better than to climb into my snug little Dart and drive away from this sadness, back to the basket chair at Union Terrace. Channel 6 is showing a movie from the late forties tonight. It's called *Roadhouse* and in it Ida Lupino sings an old sentimental ballad called "Again." She sings this in the bar of the roadhouse, casting great sultry looks at Richard Widmark, who smirks around the room, wearing one of those wide-brimmed fedoras. With any luck, I could make the last half. But neither of us will let the other go. It seems that we are as stuck with one another as husband and wife.

"I suppose the bar at The Skipper's Table would be our best bet this time of night."

"Well . . . there is a new Holiday Inn out at Richmount. Right at the end of the highway . . ."

"Yes, I've heard about that . . ."

"It's getting late, though."

"Yes."

She looks up at me with her fur-trimmed face, a regular Anastasia of the winter night.

"Would you like to come over to my place, Wes?"

"Well, yes . . . okay . . ."

"All right."

A snowflake settles on her cheek. If I were a tenderhearted lover, I would now signal this by flicking away the snowflake with a gloved thumb and smiling a smile which says that no you are not a bold person and I love your sensible plain looks and good heart Helen Corbett. Instead, I can only ask directions and wonder why the man living across the street from Harold Pendle would choose to surround his house with cold blue lights. It looks as though the Abominable Snowman should live there.

"Maybe you'd better follow me, Wes. Okay?"

"Right-o!"

She walks to a stout little Valiant two-door, her high black boots creaking in the snow. Through my window I watch her wield the long wooden scraper, looking at the back of her knees as she stretches across the hood to knock the snow from her windshield. A few minutes later finds us gone a-courting; with her in her Valiant and me in my Dart, we traverse the silent white streets of Union Place, looking through the picture windows at the bluish lights of television sets, ever watchful for the slippery street conditions and the octagonal stop signs which await us at the crossroads.

She lives on the fifteenth floor of a tall white building called The Diplomat. It's out at the north end of Napier Avenue near the Macdonald–Cartier Freeway. Standing here and looking out the living room window, I can see the running lights of the tractor-trailers sweeping across the Freeway, headed for Ottawa and Montreal. Farther out towards Bay Ridges, it is possible to detect the revolving blue light of a snow plough moving slowly westward towards the city.

Things have brightened in the last half-hour and it is not at all bad to be standing here, high above Toronto, in Helen Corbett's apartment, with a large rye and water in my hand, watching the snow fall and the traffic glide along the Freeway. In fact, it is a fine diversion for early Friday morning. Right now the hostess is freshening up in the bathroom and I am left alone to enjoy this coziness.

Along one wall is a huge stereo and I can only lift the fine grainy lid and gaze admiringly at the gleaming panel of buttons and knobs. It was built, I understand, by the boy friend of Helen's roommate—an engineer by profession.

I was wrong about Helen's living alone. Her roommate Audrey is a computer programmer and she's engaged to the engineer. According to Helen, she's spending Christmas in Nassau with two girl friends—a final fling before marriage. Graduation portraits of Audrey and the engineer stand side by side on the dresser in one of the bedrooms. Audrey has a scholar's face framed by cat's-eye glasses and long dark hair. The engineer is dark, brush-cutted and bespectacled. They could be brother and sister.

Helen has tuned in an FM station and the announcer's deep rich baritone fills the room. *And now the city sleeps. The traffic's dull roar is stilled. And we are left alone. To contemplate the night.* There follows a great soughing of violins and a chorus begins to sing an oldie called "You and the Night and the Music." The air seems suddenly charged with longing. The very molecules are a-quiver with desire. Helen Corbett stands in the doorway, leaning on one hip, looking newly washed in skirt and sweater. Now is the time to set aside the drink and take her in my arms. But I do no such thing, though what I do is every bit as good. I only raise my glass and toast her presence. It's a gallant little gesture, to be sure, spontaneous and natural, though it is possible that I saw it in a movie at one time or another. In any case, it pleases her very much and she looks coyly down at her pleated grey skirt like a convent girl.

"I hope you don't mind. I feel more comfortable."

"No, indeed. I really like it."

She walks across the room and settles herself down in front of the stereo, tucking her legs beneath her and spreading her skirt around. In this position she is able to riffle through the records, holding her head to one side, like the girl in the advertisement which says "An evening at home can be fun with . . ."

"What would you like to hear, Wes? What sort of music do you like?"

"Well, anything really. Whatever suits you."

"How about *West Side Story*? The original sound track. I know it's old, but I still think it's great."

"That's fine."

The frantic overture leaps from the speakers into the room. Helen sits there on the floor, swaying to the music and humming the melodies. She seems to know the overture by heart and can tell when the sweet tuneful parts are coming. Sitting there listening to the music, with her thick legs tucked beneath her skirt, she looks as happy as June Allyson in some old movie. I feel fine too, a dark romantic figure standing in the shadows by the window. After a moment she looks over at me and playfully rattles the ice cubes in her glass.

"Like another drink?"

"Yes, please. If you'll join me."

"Love to."

She is starting to feel impish and light-headed and when she springs to her feet she misjudges slightly and totters, breaking the fall with the palm of her hand.

"Whooops . . . take it easy, Helen old girl," she says, half to herself. We both laugh, embarrassed. Helen has been knocking back a few in the kitchen while I stood here watching the trucks roll by. Now she pads from the room in her stocking feet, her heavy tread shivering a small picture along the wall. I would hate to live under those solid footsteps.

In the darkened room we dance, holding each other around the waist like love-sick teen-agers, shuffling over the broadloom as we listen to Mr. Bernstein's colourful New York tunes. Helen Corbett nuzzles her head into my neck and closes her eyes. A few moments ago we kissed with lips that were parted and dry.

"I know you're married, Wes," she says over my shoulder. "Harold told me."

"Does it make any difference?"

"No, I don't care."

She hugs me tightly. The music swells—a lyrical passage in which a boy and girl sing of their love. Helen seems to have trouble finding her breath. She breaks apart and looks up at me with shining eyes, her fingers in the flesh of my arms.

"Oh, Wes. I want to be happy. Make me happy!"

"Aren't you happy now?"

"I don't know . . . yes."

We hold each other closely and sink to the floor. Lying there with my face pressed into her hair I can see a fluff ball under the divan. Suddenly a jet of air from the baseboard register sends it capering across the floor to a dark fugitive corner. Helen kisses me roughly on the mouth, working her tongue back and forth between my teeth. I reach under her sweater for a flat spongy breast, a palpable disappointment after Molly's great set.

". . . Wes?"

The voice seems far away.

"Yes?"

She is being tender, stroking the side of my face.

"You looked so sad and lonely at the party tonight."

"Did I?"

"I know things aren't going well in your marriage. I won't pry."

"It's all right. You're very sweet."

"Sssssh, darling."

She kisses me on the nose and sits up. Through half-closed lids I watch her reach behind to unfasten her brassiere. Then she pulls the sweater over her head and hikes up the skirt to unhook her garter belt. The dark hair falls across her face like a veil. Alas for her poor thin-shouldered body; it is an unlovely thing to gaze upon. Her thighs are fantastic, enormous white cylinders. She lies naked beside me, stroking my face.

"I wonder if my Grade Ten girls could see me now what they would think."

"What would you like them to think?"

"I don't know," she smiles. ". . . that I'm not always what they think I am."

"Do you really care what they think?"

"No, I suppose not . . . or yes, I do . . . I'm not sure."

We cling to each other and kiss. The broadloom smells faintly of feet. Helen Corbett nips at my ear lobes with her teeth and I drive my face into her throat. We thrash about on the rug like landed fish. It is no use. Her milk-white sea-cold body is an affront. In desperation I plunge my hands between her damp legs.

"Oh, touch me, Wes! Do things to me!"

"Yes."

The record changer clicks ominously in the silence.

The overture begins again.

"Oh, Wes . . . Wes . . . Wes . . . Wes . . ."

She holds my face in her burning hands. There are tears in her eyes.

"It's no good, dammit . . . no good . . . oh, why is everyone so unhappy . . . why?"

A terrible sob catches high in her throat.

"It's all right now. Take it easy . . . Do you like that? . . . there?"

"Oh, everyone is so goddam unhappy."

1 4 6.

She seizes my wrist and pulls my hand away. "Everyone."

"Now take it easy, for Christ's sakes."

She looks up and gently touches my face with her finger-tips.

"Oh, I'm sorry, Wes, really I am."

"It's all right."

She half-rises, leaning on an elbow. With a limp hand she sweeps the hair from her face.

"Can I have a cigarette, please?"

The smoke from her cigarette winds slowly towards the ceiling. We lie naked in one another's arms and talk. The talk is making Helen feel better. She has stopped crying and is quite calm now. I watch the smoke rise and scratch my right buttock.

". . . But I don't know. Audrey talks as though she and Bob were starting up a business. He is buying this. She is buying that. That's all she ever talks about. Is this what marriage is supposed to amount to? I don't know. She seems happy enough. But you can never tell with Audrey. She's much the same all the time. . . . But I don't think she's happy. Really happy. I don't even think she's looking forward to her marriage all that much. . . ."

Somewhere above us a rising outward-bound DC-8 climbs the sky with a heavy roar.

". . . and believe me . . . if I were a teen-ager today I'd do the same thing. They're absolutely right, you know, Wes. God . . . they sit in front of me. . . . And they really are incredibly beautiful kids . . . really alive and open and honest. Do you know that a lot of them are already on the pill? Well, why not? Some of their mothers supply them. Or, if not the mothers, the boy friends. . . . They always seem to have plenty of money. But, God I don't blame them! I don't blame any of them. . . . I sit there, you know, on Monday morning. Watching them come into class. Oh, I can always tell the ones who have spent a weekend making love in the Mustang or smoking marijuana. They look at me as if to say: And what did you do, Miss Corbett, play with yourself all weekend? Or curl up with a good book? And they're fifteen years old. When I was fifteen, and Lord, it was only twelve years ago, when I was fifteen it was Cokes at the school dance in the gym on Friday night. And be home by eleven. Phoning boys from pyjama parties. Really daring. They do all that now at eleven. . . . But I mean they are right. And I envy them in a way. Oh, not the crazy world they're growing into, but their openness and honesty. You know, Wes, it makes me boil, though of course I say nothing, because I'm a damn coward. But in the teachers' lounge. We sit around and drink coffee and tell each other what rotten kids they are. But we're really just jealous. That's all. Just jealous and full of spite and hateful because they're young and alive and just trying to be happy. . . . And dear silent Wes? What of you? What makes you happy?"

"I'm happy enough here."

"Are you, though?"

"Yes."

We embrace once more and stroke each other. Helen is suddenly tender again and touches me lightly on the organ.

"Do you like that?"

"Yes."

"How much?"

"Quite a bit."

"I want to kiss it."

"Dear God, yes . . ."

"Now . . . I want to kiss it now."

1 4 8.

To each his own is what I say and, dear Helen Corbett, with your wild nervous mouth all over me I can only say thanks a million. This is a treat. Molly doesn't like to do this even when her own admirable thighs are crushing my ears. Molly is a selfish person. But then so am I. We suit each other that way. Helen Corbett is a mass of dark hair over my groin. Who would have thought it?

Helen Corbett wants to be happy. Everyone in the land wants to be happy. It's a national goal. The Americans even write it into their constitution—life, liberty and the pursuit of happiness. It's a right bestowed on all—rich man, poor man, beggar man, thief, black man, yellow man, Indian chief. Give me my portion of happiness, you son of a bitch, or I'll smack you in the mouth. I demand my rights. The only problem is that it's making everyone miserable. Right now—I can only ask that this simple honest muscle in my chest keep working, as dear Helen Corbett transports me to pleasures too rich for the longing, too deep for the telling.

THE WEEKEND MAN

1.

On my way to Winchester House this morning I resolve to abandon the Peanut Butter Jar Method of early-morning decision-making. Starting next week I will begin each day with an arbitrary choice of breakfast and route to work. I am already feeling better for having made this resolution. From time to time I find it necessary to alter my daily routine. I am not at home with long-established habits. I can understand but not appreciate those persons who derive especial comfort from inserting into their daily passage through time those small peculiar rituals, like always sitting on the right side of the bus or buying the morning paper only from a news-stand on such and such a street. This is all very fine, but it never works for me. After a few weeks I discover that the right side of the bus or that particular newsstand is becoming so infected with Monday morningness that it is poisoning my entire day and leading me towards some costly diversion like throwing up my job or moving to new lodgings. This morning, as luck would have it, I drew the Jumbo Route from the Peanut Butter Jar and I am half an hour late. This reinforces my conviction that it is time for a change in morning habits.

At the corner of Mulcaster and Belvedere, I pull to a halt before the glare of a grandmother dressed in the garb of a school-crossing attendant. She holds up an orange table-tennis bat upon which is printed the word STOP and stares fiercely at me from behind her steel-framed spectacles. The postman's cap sits on the back of her good grey head at a jaunty angle, and a pair of lavender muffs protect her ears. Clearly, she is no one to be trifled with. Behind her, a troop of small boys and girls are marching solemnly across the street. Their sergeant, a pretty young woman in a forest-green duffel coat and snow boots, walks backwards, trimming the line with a practised eye. They are all no doubt on their way to Story Hour at the Public Library on Genevieve Avenue.

The Dart is balky this morning and I fear for its health: in fact, I am thinking of delivering it up to the people at one of the service centres along Britannia Road and asking them to take its pulse and lubricate its several moving parts with quality oil. As the final child reaches the sidewalk, Grandma waves me through. I start forward slowly, only to have the Dart shudder and stall. The old girl eyes me suspiciously. Of course, respectable Union Placers are long gone to their desks and tie counters, while I still wander these back streets, baggy-of-eye and shifty-looking. She doubtless has me pegged for a deviate. As the Dart finally pulls away, I note with satisfaction that she is taking down my licence number just in case. She is right. We must all do our part to keep these streets safe for our children.

The day is overcast and damp. Earlier this morning The Wake-Up Man told me that another low-pressure front is moving up across the lake from New York. At the moment a feeble sun swims overhead behind the clouds. Driving north on Britannia Road, I can just see the last of the Tom Thumb Traffic Helicopter as it churns westward through the milky sky and disappears behind the corner of the Woolcot Building.

It is nearly twenty minutes to ten when I open the side door of Winchester House. Something is amiss. The Shipping Area is deserted; half-opened cartons of books lie on the packing counters and desks, and smocks have been hurriedly flung across chairs. The place has an air of hasty departure about it, like those scenes in war movies when the Marines break down the bunker door and find the Germans gone but warm half-eaten meals still on the table. For a brief moment I panic. I have overslept and it is not Friday at all but Saturday and Molly will be furious because I didn't show up for dinner. But that is ridiculous. The Wake-Up Man told me it is Friday and besides the door is unlocked and the lights are on. The parking lot was filled with cars.

As I make my way through the building, the riddle is solved. The voice of Harry Ingram drifts down the corridors from the general office area. He is addressing the staff. When I pass the reception desk Miss Philips briefly turns her little puckish Audrey Hepburn face my way and then presses the earphone further into her dark hair as if to say: This is a serious business, so tread softly. I stand near a little knot of ball-grabbers from the Shipping Room and listen to Harry Ingram explain the big sale of Fairfax Press to Universal Electronics Corporation. Harry looks good today in his new double-breasted suit and fresh hair cut. It is little wonder that the office girls are looking at him adoringly, hanging on every word. The ball-grabbers are attentive too, standing here as solemn as new recruits. Harry gently pats the coloured hankerchief in his breast pocket and continues.

". . . and I want to emphasize to each and every one of you that our joining the Universal Electronics family is not, I'll repeat it, not, going to result in great sweeping changes either in policy or personnel. In other words, for the immediate future, this acquisition is not going to greatly affect any of your lives, only insofar as you can now consider yourselves to be members in good standing of one of the most dynamic corporate bodies in the free world. And believe me, this is something that I would like each and every one of you to think about. As most of you know, I've just come back from New York City. And while there I attended some very exciting meetings. And one of the things that struck me throughout these meetings, one of the things that really impressed me, was the pride and general all-around enthusiasm of the Universal people. These are very very dynamic individuals. They are full of ideas and excited about the whole Universal picture as regards the future. They know they are a part of a great organization. They are proud of it and they are eager for you to know more about it. I know that each and every one of you will feel this way too . . . I myself have always been optimistic about the future of Winchester House. And now that we are a part of Universal and all they stand for, I'm even more optimistic about what lies ahead. And frankly, I'd like each and every one of you, no matter what you do here at Winchester, to feel the same way."

Harry now dips his head down and coughs into his fist.

"And now I believe—correct me if I'm wrong—but I believe we're closing today at three. And a small reception is being held right here. Or have I got the wrong week?"

This is greeted by cries of "no, no" and a quick spatter of applause from the ball-grabbers and stenographers. On the other side of the room the editorial, advertising, and sales people smile benevolently at all this light-headed fun.

Harry Ingram holds up his hands like an evangelist.

". . . and there is one other thing that I'd like to mention and I would ask your co-operation . . . Some of you are going to be enjoying a few drinks this afternoon and that's fine. I'll probably do the same."

A few more laughs erupt here, but they fall away brokenly in embarrassment.

". . . but I would like each and every one of you to be very careful in driving your cars. The police have informed us—that is, all employers—that they will be conducting periodic spot checks and impaired drivers are going to jail for Christmas this year. That's the word and I'm passing it along . . . so let's each of us do our best to see that no tragedy mars this holiday season for a Winchester House employee . . . So this afternoon, enjoy yourselves by all means, but be careful. . . . Now I don't know about some of you fellows, but I'm having my wife pick me up . . . though, come to think of it, I don't know if that's such a good idea either . . ."

A fine burst of laughter all around, followed by mild courteous applause. Harry leaves the centre of the floor, shouldering his way through the people like a celebrity, smiling and greeting one and all—a popular leader and no mistake.

In the washroom Cecil White bends over the basin and cups the water in his long sensitive hands. When he brings these hands to the sides of his face the water trickles through the fingers and runs in rivulets among the wiry black hairs of his wrists. He gropes for the roller towel, pressing his face into the cloth like a man waking up painfully. Along with myself, Cecil is nursing a hangover, though each of us is too polite to comment.

Sometimes it pleases Cecil and me to leaven our discreet acquaintance with the yeast of irony. Although we would both be lost for words if left alone in a room for ten minutes, a brief chance meeting like this will often produce a sort of tangential informality so that a stranger happening upon us would probably believe we are old friends. In our suspicious courtly way we get on well together. Now he carefully dries his stained fingers on the roller towel and looks past me with his heavy sad eyes.

"And how do you like being a member of the Universal family?"

"It's too early to say, Cec, but they sound like a grand bunch."

Cecil permits himself a small smile at this and fishes in the breast pocket of his shirt for a cigarette. Soon the thick funky smoke from his blended tobacco is corroding the air. Like a heavy musk, it lingers in the wake of Cecil's presence wherever he goes in the building, its grey tentacles clinging to the walls and ceiling long after he has left. When he smokes his tough little Lucky Strikes and Camels, Cecil inhales deeply, often leaving the cigarette in his mouth and letting the smoke caress his gaunt cheeks. It rises like an evil blue mist, screwing shut one eye and giving him a sinister Mephistophelian look. The single open eye squints wisely back at you through the smoke, inviting you to amaze its master. It is a stance for the receiving of outrageous statements. Now Cecil half-hangs on the door, coughing recklessly, one hand curled around the knob like a claw.

"That grammar manuscript you brought into the house?"

"Yes?"

"I'm sending a memo to Harry about it. You'll get a copy."

"Oh?"

"Who is this fellow Pendle?"

"He teaches at Union Place Secondary."

"One of Dunc MacCauley's men?"

"Yes."

"Well . . . it looks promising."

"No kidding."

I mean my innocent American-sounding phrase to convey genuine wonder, but perhaps I don't give it the proper rising inflection. And Cecil still seems to think that I'm transmitting on our own special ironic wave-length. So he springs the door open and smiles faintly with the air of a diffident man who has already disclosed too much.

"Yes . . . no kidding," he says dryly.

The door closes with a swish of air. I may have offended him by not expressing more interest. He's a sensitive man. To tell the truth, I am entirely surprised by his news. I had imagined Harold's manuscript to be worthless. Why I assumed this leaves me puzzled. Why I continue to assume anything about anything is an even greater puzzle.

As I pass Sydney Calhoun's office, I am hailed through the open doorway.

"Hey, Wes-boy! Come in here!"

Sydney is perched on one corner of the desk, looking down at his wide tan brogues. Now he raises his legs and snaps the brogues together, like a man passing an idle moment inspecting his shoeshine. There is a touch of the dandy in the gesture. Roger MacCarthy eyes me merrily as

I walk into the office. He is leaning against the window sill, fingering the cord on the venetian blind. Ron Tuttle is leafing through a new sample text and nods his head in greeting.

These little bull sessions in Sydney's office are to be expected. Salesmen are talkative fellows who like to get together and exchange stories. It can be good for business too. Many a sound idea has been born in the joking and banter of sessions like this. Or so I read in the October issue of *The Commercial Man,* a magazine for salesmen which Sydney marks up and circulates each month. For all I know, this may be true, though no sound ideas have ever emerged from any session I've attended. Certainly, though, it is not a bad way to pass a few moments, standing here and quipping about the business while other people hammer typewriters and open dictionaries. Because it is Friday there are lively high spirits in this morning's session. Roger suddenly whacks the cord with a mighty fist and sends it flying.

"Just look at old gentleman Wes there now. He's been keeping late hours again."

Roger says this good-humouredly, giving me a fat wink into the bargain. Ron Tuttle laughs and puts the book back on the shelf. He stands there sucking a tooth and looking pleased with events. He would like to swing the talk around to Universal Electronics Corporation and the future of Winchester House. But Sydney is now gripping the edge of his desk and has leaned back so that his legs are stretched directly out in front of him. He holds this position for several seconds, his face trembling and darkening with blood. When he drops his legs the heavy shoes hit the floor with the dull crack of a rifle shot.

"Hey now! Will you look at that?" Roger cries.

"Not bad for an old middle-aged fellow, eh!" Sydney says, breathing hard through his mouth. He invites each of us to try, even suggesting a contest, but none of us is up to it.

Roger wants to talk about the office party. He is really beside himself with joy this morning, fidgeting there in a spanking new suit, living the party inside his head. I would like to help him out, perhaps deflate the pressure a little bit, but I can only stand and listen and stare at the Territory Board. The Territory Board is a large wall map of Canada upon which are stuck several coloured pins. These pins represent the salesmen and their various territories. I am the green pins.

"We were talking a few moments ago, Wes, about our basic equipment line and how inadequate it's really been. We all think that now with Universal behind us we'll really have something to show."

"I'd have to agree with that, Ron."

Ron gives me a sly little grin and hitches up his pipe-stem trousers.

"Then you're not really worried about American big business taking over the Canadian economy?"

"There are other things to worry about this morning, Ron."

All this refers to a conversation we had several weeks ago in his office. I can't remember but I must have made some remark about the Americans. I vaguely recall that my attitude upset Ron at the time, though, to be honest, I am not usually given to striking attitudes on these matters.

"You know you don't look so well this morning," Sydney says to me, leaning back in his chair. "You young fellows should take better care of yourselves. Believe me, it'll catch up with you."

Roger catches hold of the flying cord.

"Old Wes there . . . he's too busy living it up. Right, Wes?"

"By the way," Sydney says, lacing his fingers behind his

head like a village editor, "you two characters had better take notice. Our freshman salesman friend here has brought a very promising grammar manuscript into the house. According to our chief editor, it looks very good."

"Hey, that's really great, Wes, congratulations," Roger says, sending the cord into another crazy orbit.

"Yes, good work," Ron says, smiling and examining the bookshelf.

Sydney addresses the ceiling.

"And this is as good a time as any to remind ourselves that we're not only salesmen but field editors too. Take a page from Wes's book here and *read* it. We should always be scouting for new manuscripts and new manuscript ideas. Keep your eyes on the bright boys in the schools and keep reminding them that we're now plugged into Universal. As a matter of fact, I think I'll do a monthly memo on this, beginning in the new year. Just a reminder, along with a list of those subject areas where we could stand new material."

We all agree that this is a good idea.

"Okay, then . . ."

Sydney now lunges forward towards his desk, the great shoes smacking the floor again and the hands dropping flatly on the green blotter.

"Well . . . we'd better get cracking or we'll never get any work done today."

The bull session is over. As we make our way towards the door, I let the others go on ahead before asking a favour of Sydney.

"I wonder, Syd . . . I'd like to visit Andrew for a few minutes this morning. It shouldn't take long."

Sydney looks up at me in his round-faced way and then shakes his head almost sternly.

"Well, go ahead, Wes. Take as much time as you like.

For Pete's sake, you don't have to ask for something like that."

Mrs. Bruner is wearing a new green dress today and showing a nice amount of leg as she bends forward to search for something in the filing cabinet. She looks up as I pass by and flashes a smile that is full of the promise of things. I can recognize a weekend smile when I see one.

"Good morning, Mr. Wakeham."

"Good morning."

She straightens up and leans on the cabinet with a generous hip thrust out and one arm akimbo. Standing there like this, she looks as cocky as a Hamburg streetwalker. She is in a good humour this morning and is even willing to crack a few jokes at my expense.

"You don't look so well, Mr. Wakeham. Are you feeling all right?"

"Yes, I'm fine. A little tired, thank you."

"Ah . . . ah," she says, wagging a finger at me mock-serious. I am a naughty child and she is taking the liberty of scolding me. It is her notion of levity.

"These late nights, Mr. Wakeham. They will catch up with you."

"I'm sure you're right about that, Mrs. Bruner."

"Can I get you something? An aspirin?"

"No, it's all right. I'll be fine."

"There is one message for you."

She walks to her desk and looks down, her nylon stockings rustling faintly as her fine long legs brush together.

"Ah . . . a Mr. Sinclair. He called a few moments ago. He said he would call back."

"Thanks very much."

"I'll bring you some coffee."

What a blessed season of the year this is! As the storyteller says, even the stoniest hearts are open to entreaty.

The mail is light today. An order for two twelve-inch globes and a request for one copy of *Let's Discover Numbers*. Also a Christmas card from Mrs. Teale at the Fortescue School. She will doubtless wonder why I did not send her a poinsettia this year. I cannot tell her that the thought of sending a poinsettia each Christmas leaves me paralysed with gloom. When Bert Sinclair calls again, it is to invite me to Christmas dinner.

"Good morning, Wes, and Merry Christmas!"

"Yes . . . the same to you, Bert."

"And many more of them, boy. . . . How are things?"

"Fine, and thanks by the way for sending me the piece about the oil man."

"The which?"

"The clipping about Clyde R. Wheeler, the Oklahoma oil man."

"Oh, the *Digest* thing. Yes . . . did you enjoy it?"

"Yes."

"Good . . . quite a story, isn't it? Darn plucky guy. I sent it along to you, Wes, because I know you get down a bit at times. Little stories like that can sometimes lift a fellow. . . . I know you're having it rough these days. . . . Living in that apartment all by yourself. . . . Cooking your own meals. . . . And starting out in a new career at your age."

At my age! Of course when Bert was thirty he had already put in twelve years at the Boulder Corporation. From high school straight to Boulder and old Bert's been rolling along ever since.

"Say, by the by, Wes . . . the reason I called . . . Molly's told me that the two of you are having dinner tonight. Right?"

"Yes, sir."

"Good . . . now listen . . . Last night I had a long heart-to-heart with that girl of mine, and now it's your turn." He laughs.

"Are you ready for a little sermon?"

"Sure."

We both laugh.

"Okay now. Look. . . . It's Christmas time and you two kids ought to be together. It's certainly the time to put aside your little differences and try to co-operate. Have a little fun, for heaven's sake . . ."

I am silent.

"Wes? . . . I'm going to be awfully disappointed if I don't see my daughter and her husband at the dinner table on Sunday."

"Well, Bert, I don't know. . . . I'll have to see how Molly feels and . . ."

". . . it's Christmas time and you should be with your wife."

And son, Bert might have added, only mentioning Andrew is always unpleasant and Bert is not about to look for unpleasantness. He prefers to leave it in some dark corner of his mind where the broom never quite reaches.

"Well, how about it, son? Are you going to try to work this thing out tonight?"

"Well, I think we always try, Bert."

"Good boy. . . . Listen. We'll have a wonderful Christmas together. I know it. . . . How's the job coming along, by the way?"

"Fine."

"You'll do well there, Wes, I just know it. You're in a great field too. Education is just going everywhere today. It's the coming thing . . ."

"That's right."

"Well, I have to slide along now. Oh, say . . . give my best to Syd Calhoun, will you? Tell him I'm going to try and get up to the cottage over the holidays. I'll look over his place while I'm there."

"Good."

"Take care, Wes. . . . And listen, you two kids have a good time tonight, eh!"

"Right . . . and thanks, Bert."

"Fine, Wes . . . bye, bye . . ."

"Bye, bye, Bert."

2.

Mrs. Teale is waiting for me in the sun room. The very sight of her is reassuring. She's a big deep-bosomed woman with a face that should appear in this day and age on packages of frozen pies to attest to their home-baked goodness. Actually, that is the old advertising man in me talking but it is nevertheless true. From the top of her marcelled grey hair to the bottoms of her broad-heeled white oxfords she is Motherhood Itself. Whenever I talk to her, I am always prepared to surrender to her large friendly ways and let them enfold me like an old family eiderdown.

Our talk this morning is freighted with memories of seasons past. Mrs. Teale is no longer much interested in the future and this time of the year is difficult for week-enders like her. Today she is actively suffering from the *nostalgies*. Since her husband died ten years ago she has had no one to talk to about the rich full days when she was a girl on her father's farm. Therefore, when Mrs. Teale and I aren't talking about Andrew or house plants and how to grow them, she is telling me about her happy girlhood on the farm. I am probably the only human being alive who knows so much about Mrs. Teale's girlhood. If you believe I listen to these recollections out of kindness for a lonely heart, you are mistaken. I listen to them because it pleases me to be drawn backward in time and to imagine this big grey-haired woman standing next to me as a buxom young farm girl. It is a diversion we both enjoy, she in the telling and I in the listening.

Today the talk is of distant winter days on the farm. The period is the years of the Great War as Mrs. Teale calls it. One Christmas Eve an uncle's house on the next concession burned to the ground. The flames could be seen for miles. Mrs. Teale, who was fifteen at the time, drove a sleigh through most of the night, fetching relatives and friends to help the stricken family. Mrs. Teale remembers it as an awful night, by which she means that it was one of the best nights of her life. Certainly it seems to me a brave resourceful thing to have done and in my mind's eye I can see this blooming young girl at her task, urging the team of Percherons along the road under the winter sky. We are both sorry when the tale comes to an end and we must make our way along the wide bright corridor. It is like coming out of a movie house into the afternoon sunlight. As we walk along, both of us feel a little let down at the sure knowledge that nothing today will be any match for that winter night of over half a century ago.

1 6 8.

The door to the classroom is open and the children are seated on low stools. They form a circle in the centre of the room. In the middle of the circle Miss Thompson holds up coloured pictures of the Nativity and tells the children about the birth of Jesus. Most of the older ones are listening intently, their features tortured into grim concentration as they try to puzzle out the magic of the story. Others are dreamy-eyed, staring vacantly at the crayoned art work which hangs along the walls like strange vivid paintings. One dark good-looking boy is caught up entirely within himself. He sits on his stool rocking back and forth, one tight little fist pressed against his temple as though he were listening to some imaginary conversation on an old-fashioned wall telephone. Through it all he makes a low soft sound, a loveless croon as old as mourning. It is clearly distracting and at one point Miss Thompson must break off her story and look over at him. "Now, Kenneth," she says gently, "we are all here to listen to the story. You must try to be a little quieter so that others can hear."

Andrew sits quietly with his hands on his knees. It is a curious way for a small boy to sit. In its peculiar stillness and dignity the position seems to confer all the patience and wisdom of the ages upon the person assuming it. As I stand next to Mrs. Teale looking in at him, I realize suddenly and with a terrible pang that I used often to see my father sitting in this manner.

Andrew is growing as fat as a chub and seated there in his brown corduroy overalls he looks like some chunky Oriental youngster living on a commune somewhere in the heart of Asia. I stand by the door and wait while Mrs. Teale goes into the classroom and talks to Miss Thompson, who looks over my way and smiles. Soon Mrs. Teale is walking back holding Andrew's hand. He careens along beside her with an awkward rolling gait, for he has still not fully co-ordinated all his motive powers. There is a slight suggestion of a pout around his lower lip. He was enjoying the bright cheerful room and the presence of the other children. But when Mrs. Teale leaves us in his room he recovers his good nature and grins at me. He is an affectionate little fellow and likes nothing better than to play a game of noodle with me. This is a game which I invented to amuse him and we both enjoy it. It is played by placing our hands on each other's faces and bringing our heads together so that our faces actually touch. In this position I intone the single word noodle over and over and this comical incantation seems to fill him with deep delight. Sometimes when he is especially pleased with my noodling he will place his arms around my neck and lay his big head against my chest. From there he will look up at me with his narrow hooded eyes blinking solemnly into my face. Now and then and for no particular reason he will give me a tremendous grin, limning his singular message of love.

Today our noodling goes well and we both have an excellent time. When we part we hug each other tightly and without a sound but he is not really sorry to see me go. He is already anxious to get back to the classroom and the other children. In the small lobby Mrs. Teale and I stand inhaling the deep leather smell of the chairs and looking out the window at the noon traffic along Bloor Street. A radiator hisses away softly in one corner. Mrs. Teale is feeling pensive and she would like me to feel this way too but really I am in fair spirits thanks to Andrew and our noodling. Mrs. Teale, however, does not notice this and carries on in her gently doleful mood.

"It's a hard time, Mr. Wakeham. Christmas can be a hard time for some people."

"Yes, that's very true, Mrs. Teale."

"I suppose we should count our blessings but sometimes that isn't so easy either."

"No, indeed."

We both stare ahead through the window, lost in our own private griefs like solitary travellers. I find myself wishing she would talk about the condition of her new tuberous begonia. We discussed this plant at some length during my last visit. I have a mind to ask, but check myself when she shakes her head. She is diverting herself now but she is paying for it. That is one thing about diversions. They must be paid for. It's one of the great natural laws, like gravity. Mrs. Teale shakes her head again.

"When poor Frank and I . . . ah, well! . . ."

She brings her hands together and pats the sleeve of my all-weather coat. The wedding band is sunk deep into the flesh of her finger, and staring down at the plump hand, I am moved to wonder how the finger looked when her husband first placed the band there.

"I'm sure everything will work out for you, Mr. Wakeham."

"Thank you, and I hope you have a nice Christmas."

She smiles her best sweet smile of lightly worn sadness. It is a professional smile and means to win hearts.

"It's always the same now, Mr. Wakeham. I go to my sister's in Mimico. Her husband is retired, a railway conductor. They have a daughter, my only niece, but she lives in Denver, Colorado. Her husband's in the Air Force out there. They seldom come back to Toronto. I guess it's too far for them to drive. So the three of us sit around and watch television, three old fogies, I'm afraid. . . . Not much fun there. . . . Oh, you need young people around to make a Christmas."

"Well . . ."

"Don't you worry about Andrew, now. He's coming along just fine."

"Yes. He looks well, doesn't he? . . . By the way, I wonder, did Mrs. Wakeham say what time she was picking Andrew up?"

"Well, now I can't exactly recall but I believe she said about two. If there's a message you'd like me to deliver, I'd be glad to."

"No, it's all right, thank you. I'll say good-bye now."

"Yes, good-bye, Mr. Wakeham, I enjoyed our little chat. I always do."

The day is quite soggy and mild. It is a day when the backs of women's nylons are flecked with mudspots from passing cars. Overhead a drab grey sky rolls the clouds and sends them booming northward ahead of a damp wind. It is weather for Good Friday, not Christmas. I had briefly thought I might eat my lunch in one of the downtown taverns but at the last moment I decide to get out of the centre of the city and return to Union Place. I will go to the Zumburger stand in the Shopping Plaza and have two Zumburgers and a glass of milk as originally planned.

Driving east along Bloor Street towards the Parkway, I am involved in a slight altercation with the driver of a panel truck, a surly-looking, black-haired fellow. He is under the impression that I do not want him to pass my Dart. He finally pulls abreast of me at Parliament Street, where we are stopped for a red light. He leans across his cab and shouts through the open window.

"Why the fuck don't you get over, Grandpa? I got work to do."

"What's that?"

"Fuckin' dummy Sunday driver."

"Bite my arse."

3.

Although I have come to live with them, I am still bemused from time to time by the thundering ironies. Sometimes I simply have to stop whatever I'm doing and shake my head as though to clear a ringing sound. For the past fifteen minutes I have been sitting here in my office waiting for the party to begin. I have taken down *The Chain of Life* and opened it to the chapter on insects. Although I didn't particularly want to, I forced myself to read a section on *Blatta orientalis*, a tough shell-backed little creature from the order *Orthoptera*. Many of you will know him as the common cockroach. Did you also know that there are 1,200-odd species of cockroach? Now here is a peculiar thing, or so it strikes me. For some reason, *Blatta orientalis* has resisted evolution or evolution has simply passed him by. Anyway, he has crawled through time unchanged and unimproved, secreting vile odours and crushed underfoot or eaten by higher forms of life. And yet, of all God's creatures, it is lowly little *Blatta orientalis* which may prove to be the most adaptable. I learned all this from a television programme called *Science and You* which I sometimes watch on Sunday afternoons. Now whenever I think about it I fall into a state of mild bemusement.

The host of this programme is a cheerful little man, a biologist by profession and something of a comedian too. He enjoys making little jokes on subjects you wouldn't normally think all that funny. Standing there in his white lab coat with the slide rule and ball pen in the breast pocket, he reminds me of those doctors and dentists who handle themselves in this manner, telling you funny little stories while they plunge a needle into your arm or drill a back tooth. It is a style calculated to put you at ease with the serious business of experts. During his talk on *Blatta orientalis*, the biologist held up a beaker and gave it a few shakes so that we could all see the black bug imprisoned within. *Do you see this little fellow?* he asked with that knowing grin that says I am about to let you in on something remarkable. *This is Blatta orientalis, one of the toughest and most durable creatures roaming the planet. Why do I say tough and durable? Well . . . should we humans ever be foolish enough to engage in all-out thermonuclear war* [small smile], *I'm afraid it will not be the meek who will inherit the earth.* [Pause and smile.] *No, indeed.* [Shaking the beaker again and looking almost fondly at the bug.] *It will be our little friend here—Blatta orientalis of the order Orthoptera, together, of course, with his 1,200-odd cousins.*

That in any case seems to be the consensus among scientists studying the effects of radiation on the animal world. Something to think about, eh!

But thinking about *Blatta orientalis* is as bad as thinking about the Monday and Wednesday mornings of January and March. The only thing for it is diversion. If I can just sit still and wait for the party. However, that is no good either, for I am soon trapped into a fantasy in which a bold Gerta Bruner and I slip away from the others and have sexual congress in this office. I bend her backwards across this very desk and take her like a Goth of old. No—thinking about the party is the worst thing to do.

It turns out that I am rescued by none other than Mrs. Bruner herself, who enters the office bearing a cup of tea and a macaroon. She is still in a fine humour and like many big women when they are happy she tends to flounce her body a bit, throwing out a fair amount of hip as she moves across the room with a swaying motion. Molly used to do this in the bedchamber when she was in a jubilant mood, exaggerating the sway until it became whorish and funny. Mrs. Bruner places the tea on my desk and looks down at the open book.

"Early tea today, Mr. Wakeham."

"Excellent."

Mrs. Bruner would like to stay and chat awhile. She has finished up her work for the day and is now waiting for three o'clock. Her desk will be as bare and clean as a surgeon's table. The other salesmen must be occupied, for I am the last person she seeks out when time lies heavy on her hands. Now she smiles. It amuses her to be tolerant and sisterly towards me today.

"How is the head feeling now?"

"Oh, much better, thanks. I'm going to make it."

She laughs, throwing back her head—a hearty Teutonic chuckle. "Ah, good. I'm glad."

Without saying as much, we decide to be pleasant to one another and we talk about the holidays. She and Helmut are going to the Tannenbaum Dance at the German Club tonight. Last year they won a door prize—a dozen bottles of Löwenbräu. She does not think they will be so lucky this year, though I tell her that I hope they are, for Löwenbräu is an excellent brew, the finest, in fact. This pleases her no end, and we part the best of comrades.

When she leaves I decide to call Molly in the hope that she will be back from the school. She never said whether she was going to make the reservations at Martino's or expected me to do this. If we arrive there tonight without reservations and cannot get seated, our evening will be off to a bad start. When the call rings through, it is Molly's mother who answers and this presents me with the familiar problem of how to address her. Mother or any variation of the word is out of the question and Mildred is too familiar: she would never stand for it. I usually end up sparring around and calling her nothing. Her voice on this December Friday is as crisp as new money.

"Yes?"

"Hello."

"Yes?"

"Can I speak to Molly, please?"

"Is that you, Wesley?"

"Yes."

"Molly's at the school now picking up Andrew. Is there any message?"

Whenever we talk, Mildred bristles like a porcupine.

"Well, no. I guess not. It's all right. I'll see her tonight. Thanks anyway . . ."

Mildred hangs up without a word. I do what I should have done in the first place—call Martino's and speak to a pleasant Mediterranean gent. He tells me that a table for Mr. and Mrs. Wakeham has already been reserved for eight o'clock.

4.

Friday afternoon is the best part of the weekend and now the general office area of Winchester House is filled with people who are merry as crickets. I am with them all the way as I drink beer and listen to Ron Tuttle and Sydney Calhoun mildly argue the best way to promote the Tele-Visor Series 40 Projector. Apparently the East Africa Atlas Give-Away isn't working all that well and sales thus far have been disappointing. Ron would like to see us offer an increased discount over a limited period in the hope of attracting more volume, while Sydney thinks that a snappy brochure mailed to all A & B schools will do the trick. As usual, I praise both schemes but champion neither, preferring to see virtue in both approaches. I sometimes feel that this is what my call in life really is—to stand around with drink in hand, looking pleasant and making people happy by agreeing with them. I have noticed, however, that no one is all that interested in my opinion unless, of course, it happens to agree with theirs, in which case they welcome it with smiles of rare fellowship. It is during this talk that Harry Ingram comes upon us. Suddenly Harry is there between Ron and me with his arms around our shoulders. He is freshly shaven and his cheeks give off the rich fragrance of spices and balm. Leaning in on his arms, he dips his sleek head into our circle and stands there like a fraternity man.

"Well, now . . . Here's the very heart of the operation itself . . . How's it going, fellows?"

Harry delivers all this without a trace of irony. He really believes we are the heart of the operation. He was a salesman once himself. Now he looks around.

"Say, where's big Rog, anyway? . . . Uh, huh . . . Over with the girls, eh!"

It is true. Roger MacCarthy, red of face and sweating like a drayman, is talking to three or four girls from the Order Department. Between great swallows of beer he is telling them jokes and making them laugh.

"So now . . . what do you fellows think of the big news?" Harry asks, grinning at each of us. We all think it promises greatly for the future and Harry decides to get serious about it. His face becomes stone solemn and he drops his hands from our shoulders, the better to spell things out.

"Listen . . . this is the best thing that could happen to Winchester House and you guys are going to be the big winners. . . . You know eighty per cent of Universal executive comes directly out of sales.

"Look . . ."

Harry talks quietly, drawing us in towards him. We might be listening to a risqué tale the way we are bunched together. As he sells us on the advantages of membership in the Universal family, Harry uses his hands to keep score of the good things that are going to accrue, uncurling a finger from his left hand each time and tapping it with his right forefinger.

"Two: as far as management possibilities, the sky's the limit. Remember Universal is a world-wide organization. Why, you fellows could even end up in some sunny place like Hawaii. . . . Three: better all-round security within the corporate structure. . . ."

As Harry talks, two thoughts occur to me. One, he is talking only to Ron and me. Sydney is listening and nodding his head in agreement, but Harry has already been given the word that Sydney Calhoun does not figure in Universal's plans for the future. Two, Harry himself is really shaken by all this and, as a matter of fact, is frightened as hell. It's soon time for him to move along and reassure others. Before he goes, though, he puts his arm around my shoulders again and gives me a good shaking.

"Hey, Syd! Where did you get this guy, anyway?" he asks, serious-faced.

Sydney regards us warily. "Get him?"

After all these years he is still not on to this simple feature of Harry's style—the loaded question that turns itself into a compliment.

Harry gives me another good shaking in the shoulders. "Well, wherever you got him I wish you'd find me three more. Did you see Cecil White's memo? The rookie here has brought in what sounds like a very excellent property."

Sydney's melon face is lighted by a regular sunburst of

a smile, a smile that is filled with immense beneficence and good will. I have no doubt but that Sydney would lay down his life for me this very moment.

"Yes, I got a copy, Harry. It sounds good, doesn't it? I was just telling Ron and Roger this morning. This is what we pay them for, eh! This is part of their job too!"

"Right."

Ron Tuttle stares hard at the floor with that pouty look of a man ignored. Right now he is pondering anew the vagaries of cosmic justice, and I, for one, don't blame him. It would seem that I am going to ride to some kind of minor success on Harold Pendle's tartan coattails and Ron knows only too well that I don't deserve any of it.

"You fellows have a good Christmas now, eh! Relax and enjoy yourselves. Syd, I'll bet you a lunch you put on ten pounds."

Harry slides away towards another group and the people step respectfully aside to admit him. He is soon telling them about the good things coming up.

Sydney and Ron begin to talk about the spring promotion of a new geography series, but I excuse myself. Charley Smith is beckoning me from a corner of the room where he stands by himself sipping beer and looking around with that permanent scowl he wears on his sharp little face. Charley is in his early fifties, a small thin man with a wide mouth and hard blue eyes. He works in the Shipping Department, and as I often go through there on my way to the office, we have taken to passing the time of day. One Friday afternoon we drank some beer together in the Union Arms Hotel over on Melina Crescent and Charley gave me his life history.

It seems that he came out to Canada from England in the thirties to look for work. He had some bad luck until the war came along and he returned to England to join the army, leaving a wife and two daughters in Canada. When he came back he found his wife had taken up with another man and his two daughters didn't know him, so he started to drink heavily and drifted from one job to another. Once he joined the Communist Party and another time the Pentecostal Church, but he lost faith in both and soon left in disappointment. Now he spends most of his spare time drinking draught beer and discussing the major problems of the day. He is what is known to some people as a beverage room lawyer. Charley likes me because I don't mind listening to his theories on how the world can be made a better place to live in.

Today he's back from a beery lunch at the Union Arms and his face is mottled and swollen with anger. He is in a fine rage, though he greets me cheerfully enough.

"Hello, Wes. How's it going, my boy?"

"Hi, Charley. How are things?"

Charley pushes his face up next to mine and whispers hoarsely. "Well, the buggers are gonna stick it into us now, eh! Not that you have to worry, with your fancy college education . . ."

"How is that, Charley?"

He shakes his head from side to side in disgust, as though my obtuseness were putting the ultimate strain on his patience.

". . . these Universal big shots . . . ahhhhh, you can see it comin' . . . plain as day . . . They'll be up here in another few weeks with their bloody time-study men . . . First thing you know phfttt . . . bloody computers all over the place. . . . An' Charley Smith is out walkin' the streets . . . the bloody Depression all over again . . ."

He jabs a thumb at his chest. "Only I'm fifty-three now, my fine young friend. An' who the bloody hell . . . now I'm askin' you . . . who the bloody hell is goin' hire a bloke who's fifty-three in this day and age . . ."

"Oh, I don't know, Charley. Why not wait and see? There may not be that many changes. Anyway, they'll make room for you."

This remark triggers an act which Charley always performs to express his contempt for innocence. It begins with a short bitter laugh followed by more head shaking and the laying of a skinny grey hand on my shoulder. Then he proceeds to take hold of my outrageous statement and give it such a battering that the words fall away from the sentence like fruit from a storm-swept tree.

". . . find room for me," he whispers, savagely looking around the room with wild eyes. "Oh, that's bloody rich, my son. An' me belongin' to no union. Oh, they'll find room for me all right . . . you'll find me out on the bloody street, that's where you'll find me . . . there's plenty of room out there . . ."

I shift around on my feet and look gravely out over the faces in the room, locking my jaws together and setting my cheek muscles to work. With my arms folded across my chest and my weight slung on to one hip, I can stand here next to Charley as grim-faced as a Depression dirt farmer. But really, it is the only thing to do. Charley is in a bad way this afternoon.

"Ah shit . . . It's the same all over. The big boys are takin' over and they're just pushin' the little man aside. It's the way of things . . ."

He pauses for a swig of beer, tipping his head back and letting his skinny throat work hard to get it all down.

"How old are you, son?"

"Thirty."

"Ahhh, thirty. . . . Well, listen here to me now . . . when

I was thirty I was stickin' my neck out, see . . . servin' in His Majesty's Forces with the Eighth in North Africa. Not that I minded. I figured it was my duty and I did it . . . chasin' Jerries across the desert. Yes, I did it and I'm proud I did. . . . Ahhh, it doesn't matter a damn. . . . Still, it gets you when you see them over here with fancy jobs and handin' out all sorts of dirt too. . . . Livin' like kings and twenty-five years ago they was runnin' across the desert, every man jack of 'em, like a pack of bloody dogs. . . ."

I have heard all this before. Charley is now about to come down hard on Germans and Italians, especially those Germans and Italians who emigrated to Canada and now have good jobs or businesses, with fine homes and polished automobiles sitting in the driveways. I ask him if he would like another beer but he merely shakes his head and falls into a deep angry silence.

The party is gathering its own momentum and people are beginning to talk louder to make themselves heard. The young stenographers and filing clerks are casting off their shyness and trading jokes with their bosses. Roger Mac-Carthy still has several girls around him, including the incomparable Shirley Pendergast, who stands right up next to him. Now she is the sexiest-looking girl and it is enough to make a man go all sweaty and a-tremble just gaping at her in those spiky-heeled shoes and tight-knit dress. She is too fabulous a piece altogether and I swear I don't know how Roger can stand being so close to her like that. He stands there with his tie loosened and his shirt unbuttoned at the top. He is telling a story in which it is necessary for him to talk like Donald Duck. It is convulsing Shirley.

Rosemary Prewitt is leaning against a wall, bouncing off it actually in a casual sort of way, as she talks to Cecil White's young editor friend, Tim. They are having a cozy chat. I have noticed that girls like Rosemary often have a great deal to say to effeminate men. In school and college you could always see these girls gathered around some fragile young man talking about Bertolt Brecht or Eugène Ionesco. Now, though, they are talking about furniture and design. Tim has just moved into a new apartment and he is clearly excited at the prospect of decorating it. He is dressed in a yellow Nehru jacket and green bell-bottom trousers. When he waves his soft pale hands through the air he reminds me of a languid young hairdresser from one of the smart downtown salons. However, I make him nervous and he becomes as bashful as a young girl stammering out the words and flushing deeply to the roots of his long fair hair. He can scarcely utter an intelligible sentence with me standing around. And so I smile and withdraw, for I will not have anyone nervous on my account even though, on balance, I would rather hear Tim tell me about his new apartment than listen to Charley Smith or, yes—gape at Shirley Pendergast's fantastic arse.

When last I saw her, Mrs. Bruner was telling Dorothy Lovitt about her encounter with the black man. I've heard her tell it many times. It so happened that several weeks ago on her way home from night school Mrs. Bruner chanced to find herself on an empty bus with a black man. This was out on Junction Road, a dark strip of highway that cuts across the north end of Union Place near the Freeway. I've driven along it many times on my way to suburban schools to the north. The area is not yet fully developed, though a man named Lucas is building a house a day up there. In any case, that's what the signs along Junction Road say: "Sam Lucas. Home Contracting. Another Lucas Comfort-King Home Was Built Today." Most of these houses still stand deserted and ghostly along the

1 8 5.

winter road. Mrs. Bruner is right. It is sinister and weird late at night up in that neck of the woods. Shortly after Mrs. Bruner was seated this night, the bus stopped to admit a strong-looking, very black young Negro man (to use Mrs. Bruner's words). This man stepped aboard and—wouldn't you know it—walked the entire length of the bus to sit down opposite her on one of those long seats which face the aisle. Nor was this all! At the corner of Junction Road and Centennial Avenue the driver stopped the bus and went into a solitary all-night restaurant for a cup of coffee. While he was gone Mrs. Bruner read from her literature anthology, but she could tell the fellow was staring hard at her handsome legs. After a few moments he even tried to strike up a conversation, but Mrs. Bruner kept her eyes fixedly on the literature anthology and said not a word. She will tell you that she breathed more easily when the driver returned with his Dixie cup of coffee. I am almost certain that Dorothy Lovitt is the only person in our end of the building who has not heard Mrs. Bruner recall her little adventure with the black man. And this for the reason that Mrs. Bruner and Dorothy Lovitt can't stomach the sight of one another when dead cold sober.

Mrs. Bruner is not dead cold sober now but stands beside me tapping the rim of her glass against her teeth. She is amused by something and looks me over with a faint mocking smile around the corners of her mouth. The sherry has charged her face with high colour and left her in a teasing mood. I fear I am in for it. Her upper lip is moist with a fine amber film and a heavy sweet smell surrounds her like musk. I recognize it as a perfume Molly used to wear, something called Tabu. When Mrs. Bruner drains off the last of her sherry it is to look me fair in the eye like a sailor's girl.

1 8 6.

"I am told you are quite the ladies' man, Mr. Wakeham."

"Absolutely untrue."

"Yes, it is true, now. I have heard many stories. You have this reputation, you know."

"All I can say is fantastic. I live like a monk, actually."

"Ho, ho, ho, Mr. Wakeham."

"Ho, ho, ho, indeed. 'Tis all true, Mrs. Bruner, I'm sorry to say."

"Well, I think you are a very naughty man to lie to me like this."

She leans forward at a crazy angle. "Come now . . . tell me about your many mistresses . . ."

Roger MacCarthy has been filling her head with fantasies about me and now I can only shake my head and smile a weary sort of smile—one of my best smiles, I think. Mrs. Bruner decides to be, of all things, coy. She holds the glass against her jaw and grins—an outlandish grimace full of exaggerated coquetry and flounce. In all of whoredom there never was a grin like this! She holds the glass by the stem and waggles it in front of me.

"Would you get a lady another drink, Mr. Wakeham?"

"Yes, of course. With pleasure."

They have set up a bar along one side of the room and now it is three deep with people. There's a fair amount of horseplay going on here among the Shipping Department boys, who stand together near the bar. The younger ones like to push the hair back from their faces and dig each other in the ribs with their elbows while they watch the girls rustle softly by in their crisp new dresses. Charley Smith is wedged between two young fellows and is lecturing them on something or other. The office manager, Fred Curry, is looking around nervously and glancing at his watch from time to time. He's worried about all this and will only relax when the cleaning people arrive to clear away the mess.

When I return with the glass of sherry Mrs. Bruner is nowhere to be found, but I am seized by the maddest of impulses. It is the easiest thing to slip away down the corridor to the door of my little office. And son of a bitch but she is there, leaning back on her hands against the desk and grinning out at me like a big alley cat. When I hand her the sherry she sips at it and places the glass on the desk before tapping me slowly on the chest with a forefinger. It is a gesture at once familiar and bold. We might be old chums at a class reunion about to resume an ancient quarrel.

"I think we should have a nice little talk, Mr. Wakeham."

"All right. What shall we talk about?"

"I think you have been most unkind to me."

"Well, I certainly haven't meant . . ."

"No, really. It is all true. You are a very rude young man at times, and conceited too. It has to be said . . ."

She watches me carefully. It is her style to hector like this but she does not really want me to fight with her.

"You have often hurt me with your abrupt ways . . . yesterday, for example . . ."

"I am sorry about that."

"You know, at first I did not like you very much . . . and for the longest time . . ."

"Oh, really?"

"Yes. It is true," she says, taking up her glass and drinking.

"But I have come to think that beneath all this . . . this rudeness and arrogance . . . you are probably a very nice young man after all."

1 8 8.

"Thank you."

"And I think we should . . . make an oath to get along better in the new year . . . our New Year's resolution . . ."

"Good idea."

"Here, now . . . you must drink to that . . ."

She holds the glass to my mouth and I take the sweet syrupy liquid like a child.

"And now—" she closes one eye and gives me the slyest of looks, a look full of outright mischief and dalliance— "you must give me my Christmas kiss, eh!"

"Ahhh, yes . . ."

But she does not mean for me to brush these sherry-scented lips against her cheek but smack full dab on the mouth, and a fine hot open-mouthed kiss it is too, full of searching tongues and wild warm air a-mingling in our throats! Really we find ourselves locked together in the most stormy embrace, groping into each other's mouths like teenagers. She pushes her long groin into mine while I clutch her corseted bottom and hang on for dear life. Mrs. Bruner is as horny as a stoat and I can feel her big breasts against my shirt front. However, she must be encased in whalebone, for her rump is as hard as a granite wall and it is in vain that my fingers seek out yielding flesh. And so in this quick flagrant ardour we muzzle each other for the longest time, pressed against my steel-top desk. An amazing turn of events! When we finally break away from each other's grasp, though, it is plain that Mrs. Bruner is not about to suffer amazement. She is too clear-headed for any of that and her pale grey eyes, though cloudy, are frank and skeptical. She even sounds half-angry about it all.

"There now . . . how did you like that?"

"I like that fine," I say, clearing my throat. "Very nice. You're quite a woman."

1 8 9.

"Ha, ha, ha."

We are holding each other at arm's length like lovers meeting after a long absence.

"Yes, you really are. I think you've misjudged me, though. Come here now . . ."

I draw her towards me and place a hand on her breast. She smiles wanly and pushes it away.

"Oh no, now. . . . Let's not get carried too far, eh!"

"Why not? You're teasing me here."

"Oh, come now, Mr. Wakeham. I am not one of your little mistresses. . . . You can't play with me like this . . ."

"What are you talking about?"

She laughs. "I think you are probably an evil person."

She holds my face in her hands and kisses me harshly. Our teeth come together with a hollow clack as she grinds her mouth to mine. Mrs. Bruner knows a thing or two and she's probably tough and tricky in the sack. Poor Helmut! I have a fleeting vision of Mrs. Bruner returned home from the Tannenbaum Dance tonight—full of schnapps and Löwenbräu, shedding her Christmas green dress and unstaying the cords of her armour, her soft opulent body overflowing its bounds, a feast of pale trembling flesh for the television repairman. In a small fever I thrust my hand beneath her dress. It is warm and damp there but, alas, it too is sheathed in bony wrapping. The woman is as tenable as a lobster. She twists her mouth away and grabs my wrist with a firm hand.

"All right, all right, that will do now . . . a little control here, Mr. Wakeham, if you please . . ."

We are both breathing like sprinters.

"You do not have to prove what a great lover you are. It is . . . not necessary . . ." She reaches for her purse and snaps it open—a sharp peremptory action that seems laden with menace. "You do not have to grab at me like a dock-man."

"I'm sorry."

Standing there, she watches me out of the corner of her eye, dabbing on the powder with deft strokes, enjoying this role of the cool European lady. We are standing somewhat apart like this, sizing each other up, when the racket starts in the outer office. It begins with a shout and then a great splintering sound like the fall of a crashing chair.

"Good Lord! What's that?"

"I don't know."

The commotion sounds fierce—dozens of feet stampeding across open floor.

"What can that be, now?"

"I don't know, but let's stay for a while."

I reach out to her but she slips around me like a subway traveller, neatly dropping lipstick and compact into her purse.

"Let's find out what's going on out there."

She is flushed with excitement and plucks the glass off the desk with a triumphant flourish. Smiling brilliantly, she touches a forefinger to my lips.

"Give me thirty seconds and then you follow. . . . And be a good boy and don't tell anyone about this, eh!"

She downs her sherry in one good gulp and walks swiftly across the room to open the door a few inches. Standing there, she looks through the opening like a spy in the movies and then disappears, closing the door softly behind her: the beautiful ripe *Hausfrau* leaving the young lieu-tenant's hotel room. I stare dutifully at my Timex like a commando, watching the tiny hand sweep away the sec-onds.

Charley Smith stands alone in a circle of people, glaring

around the room, the cold clean light of hatred shining in his eyes. Charley is the best hater I know and looks the part. Violence has sobered him and left behind a smouldering rage. It is consuming his viscera, this rage—has doubtless already turned his insides to charcoal and now burns away soundlessly at the rest of his taut little body, reddening his neck and face. It would not surprise me to see him actually ignite like a Roman candle, flaring into angry heat until at last his troubled spirit is borne away on the strongly beating wings of the dark angel and only a small heap of grey ash remains. Here on the smoke-house floor lie the odds and ends of Charley Smith, a good hater in his time. *Requiescat in pace.*

Certain it is, though, that while I was playing amatory games, clutching and grabbing Mrs. Bruner's backside as though my very life depended on it, certain it is that Charley Smith was disturbing the waters with his heavy boatload of grievances. Only now he has taken a punch in the mouth for his troubles. I should go to his side, treat him with a bit of rough humour and whisper into his ear to settle down. I am one of the few around who can pull this off. Charley would listen to me. I am a college man but I know he finds me not a bad fellow. He would gladly have me seek him out, lay a hand on his shoulder, and invite him for a beer in the Union Arms, there to sit through the afternoon and listen to his story.

In an hour or so Charley will be ready for another ramble through his bitter past, a crazy three-wheeled journey down the corridors of his life with its narrow grimy streets of childhood London, the heaving grey sadness of the North Atlantic in February 1932, and the freezing cement of Canadian cities, the cheap glitter of the Saturday night dance-hall where he met his unfaithful wife and the grim brief glories of the desert war (hands down—the best time of all—oh, roll out that barrel again, boys!). All the exploded dreams, the rendering heart-sore rag-tag confessions of a weekend man.

I do not go to Charley's side. I watch instead from the edge of the crowd like a fugitive and carefully avoid his eyes. If the truth were known, I would rather be back in my office with Gerta Bruner than talk to Charley Smith. The man he has been quarrelling with is a newcomer to Winchester House, Christmas help. He's a tall stoop-shouldered man in his late thirties. He is a pale shifty-eyed character and looks to have spent some time in prison. He wraps books in the Shipping Department, standing in his smock at a long counter, talking and smiling out of the side of his mouth. Now he stands around with an ironic expression on his lean grey face, shrugging his shoulders and looking across at his fellow workers. *I was just standing here. It has nothing to do with me.* He looks like one of those car-accident victims, the passenger who stands around afterwards, trying hard not to be stared at by the spectators.

Fred Curry steps forward and talks to Charley. Fred's a thin bone-hard man with elastic armbands on the sleeves of his striped shirts, an honest old-fashioned martinet who has pretty much ignored the smooth corporate style. In another place and time he might have been the parish beadle. His days at Winchester House are probably numbered. The slick young New Yorkers who will fly up here next month will take one look and decide that Fred Curry is as quaint as a steam locomotive. They'll make it worth his while to get out. At the moment, however, he's very much in charge, talking to Charley in a low voice and guiding him through the door. Harry Ingram is nowhere to be seen. No doubt he's already flashing along the Parkway in his Wildcat, seated beside his lovely blond wife, thinking and worrying about his future.

The fight has damaged the spirit of the party and most people are prepared to call it a day. Many are already wearing coats and hats and offering season's greetings. Roger MacCarthy and I stand by one of the broad windows overlooking Britannia Road, watching the rain beat off the pavement. This rain has taken away the last of the snow and left Union Place the colour of an old bruise. Its dark-brown streets now stand waiting in the drizzle for nightfall. Roger sips beer and stares moodily out the window. At this hour his face is lumpish and sulky with disappointment. He is beginning to take on his dark-browed detective look. Roger wants to keep the party going and for the past half hour he's been trying to interest a few people in going with him to the bar at The Skipper's Table. It seems, though, that everyone has made other plans—last-minute Christmas shopping and the like. Roger is plainly irritated by it all.

"Well . . . what do you say, Wes?" he asks testily. "A couple more isn't going to kill us. The Table should be fun this afternoon. You know those office buildings on Melina are loaded with females. They all flock to the Table on Friday afternoons. We'll stay for an hour or so. What do you say?"

"Well now, I'd like that very much, Roger, really. But I just can't tonight. I have to go home and change. I have to go out to dinner."

"Okay . . . okay . . . it was only a suggestion." He shrugs his big shoulders elaborately.

Through the streaked window we watch Shirley Pendergast clatter down the front steps in her spiky-heeled shoes and hip-length coat, running to get out of the rain. Her tough-looking boy friend sits behind the wheel of his rusty old Ford convertible and smokes a cigarette while she climbs in beside him. He doesn't even remove the cigarette from his mouth when she leans over and plants a kiss firm on his cheek. Oh Lord—a very cool customer! What has he got? Roger would like to know the answer to that question, and for that matter, so would I. The Ford moves off, two jets of violet exhaust pluming into the mild wet air.

When I take my leave, there are only about a dozen left standing around in small clusters. Fred Curry walks back and forth smiling and rubbing his hands with a washing motion. He'll be glad to see the last of us. The two bartenders, brisk and businesslike in their stiff white jackets, are quickly filling cases with empty bottles and scraping the chip crumbs from the tablecloth with long wooden paddles. They are enjoying their work and talk to each other softly in a foreign language I can't identify. Roger stands beside Mrs. Bruner and Sydney Calhoun and a young quiet girl from the Advertising Department. They are finishing up their drinks and are all dressed to go. Sydney waves to me.

"You take it easy over the holidays, young fella, and give my best to the family."

The others look up. Mrs. Bruner smiles mysteriously. She has taken me down a peg or two today. Roger grins. He seems to be recovering his good humour and is already having a time thinking about the weekend.

He calls out to me as I go. "I hope Santa is good to you tonight, Wes, ho, ho, ho."

"Oh yes, indeed. Good-bye. Merry Christmas. Yes . . . good-bye, all . . ."

5.

I am on my way to Union Terrace in the Dart when I am strongly affected by a sense of the past: the early nineteen-forties, the war years in old Middlesburgh. It happens at the corner of Britannia Road and Prospect where I am stopped for a red light. Through my windshield I watch five teen-aged girls running. They have come down Prospect Street from Union Place Secondary School and now run across in front of me, stiff-hipped and pigeon-toed, holding their books to their chests. They are making for the restaurant next to the Pix Theatre. Watching them, I am overcome by haunted feelings, touched by fragments of the past. It is *déjà vu* for certain, but also something else, something deeper and stronger. Within me thrives the keenest sense of time and place. I seem able to reach out and feel the texture of those days: the high-school girls in their plaid skirts and bulky white sweaters, their ankle socks and brown and white saddle shoes. I have half a mind to abandon the Dart and follow them into the restaurant, ask if their mothers didn't once grow up in Middlesburgh, Ontario. It's all here at the corner of Britannia Road and Prospect at a quarter of five on a winter afternoon—this lost time, figured forth now in an *ambience* as resonant and palpable as an old sepia rotogravure. The sadness of it is suffocating. A spectacular case of the *nostalgies*!

6.

I am late for dinner with Molly. Although I left Union Terrace in plenty of time to reach downtown, I didn't reckon on the accident which slowed everything along the Parkway. When I pass the scene the police are busy winching up a spavined Mustang from down the steep embankment. The sporty little car is lifted, wavering on the cables, its sleek grey flanks cleanly stove in and raked by gravel, its handsome curving windshield spiderwebbed. A sorry sight! What the insurance people call a complete write-off. So, what with this accident and the sluggish crosstown traffic, I reach Martino's a full twenty minutes late. Standing next to the cigarette counter I speak to the maître d', a tall man with a sagging, deeply lined face. He has a serious manner and looks like one of those dark dignified young men who open the doors of Cadillacs at west-end Italian funerals. He listens without smiling and then leads me down an aisle of the crowded restaurant towards Molly's table.

I'm not surprised that Molly chose Martino's for our talk and it leaves me hopeful that she is not as serious about the divorce as she lets on. Although Molly is acting tough and cool these days, she is really as sentimental as her father. If she took after Mildred, we would be having this conversation at a table in Simpson's cafeteria or in a lawyer's office, Christmas or no Christmas. Molly and I used to come often to Martino's and the place has certain nostalgic affinities. During our courtship and for several months after our marriage we patronized it once or twice a month. I came to acquire a genuine taste for Italian food, though Molly was pregnant and had to watch what she ate. She thought the place had a romantic atmosphere and she liked to sit in one of the rear booths and look across the red-checked tablecloth at me or lean forward on her elbows and gaze into the flame of the candle lamp. It used to make me nervous when she leaned forward and started gazing into the flame of the candle lamp. It always meant that she was about to discuss our future.

In those days Molly was straight out of Victoria College, a big blooming girl, fresh and clean, with her father's large good looks. On summer days I watched with dry throat as she flexed her calves on the diving board in front of Bert's cottage, freckled and tanned and strong of thigh. When she sprang for the water it was all I could do to keep still. In Martino's she would sit opposite me and conjure up a picture of our future. In this way she put me in mind of Karen Schulyer, though Molly had a livelier imagination and could always be called upon to furnish pleasant details. There I was, seated at the head of the table, slicing the rare roast beef and passing the plates to my several children, frowning like a patriarch at any high jinks, a lean dark man and the youngest director in the history of the Boulder Corporation. After dinner I would read to the children, one chapter from *Through the Looking Glass*, and then escort them up the stairs to beddy-byes. My wife and I would then take coffee and brandy in the library and retire early for creative love-making. All this Molly would set forth with slack deliberateness: there was never a trace of breathlessness or gee-whizzery about any of it. *These things are going to come to pass, Wes. Why, it's ridiculous to think they won't.* At times like that, the only thing I could do was put my hands under the table and squeeze her big athletic knees.

In the passing of five years Molly has not entirely abandoned these hopes. She is still determined to find her happiness, whatever the cost. But living in the same house with her mother has made her more calculating. Mildred is a tough shrewd woman and can teach a girl like Molly plenty of tricks. Probably, if she hadn't spent her childhood on the playing fields of St. Helen's, Molly would have turned out a crafty person. I know that whenever she came back to live with me after a spell in the house on Brattle Street she was downright devious, scheming like a Levantine trader to win her way. This might last for several weeks, and then the guile would desert her in a crisis and she would commence to swear and cry and carry on like olden times.

In the passing of five years Molly has taken care of herself. She's really better-looking now than when I married her. The tennis games and ski weekends with Ernestine Hough and friends have kept her in trim. She dresses well too. Molly has excellent taste in clothes and Bert has seen to it that she always gets what she wants. When we moved into our first apartment I could only marvel as I dragged the clothes through the door: evening gowns and cocktail dresses, housecoats and lounging pyjamas, sports slacks and sweaters, coats of all description and jackets for all seasons. In frank amazement I counted thirty-two boxes of shoes. One day, in a rare fit of housekeeping, Molly decided to reduce her wardrobe and we spent the evening packing cartons with cast-offs for the needy and downtrodden. The next morning two men from the Salvation Army truck arrived, rough-looking birds with thin exhausted faces. They lugged away the cartons without a word. Molly was furious when I suggested that some fellow down on Sackville Street was in for a big surprise when he arrived home that night and found his wife waiting for him in a black chiffon negligee.

"And why shouldn't those people have a little elegance in their lives too?" Molly cried from the bathroom, where she was scrubbing her teeth. "You can be such a damn snob, Wes."

I listened as she spat hard into the basin, a flat angry sound like a slap on the cheekbone.

Seated at a corner table in Martino's, Molly is handsome to behold. She's dressed in a discreet grey suit (ideal for negotiation) with a flame of crimson scarf tucked in around her throat like a foulard. She's been to the hairdresser's, too, and her hair is swept up along her neck and piled high in a party fashion. Molly looks swanky and would turn the head of any man tonight. She's what my Uncle Fred, my mother's slightly seedy brother, would call "a real looker." At the moment she is giving a waiter the business. I know this routine. He has been tardy or the martini isn't dry enough and Molly finds it necessary to offer rebuke. She will dress him down quietly and in a style somewhat reminiscent of a novel by John Galsworthy. At such times she is apt to use a few old-fashioned English verbal formations such as "I should like" or "I dare say" and odd antediluvian adjectives like "lamentable" and "dreadful." Molly can be a perfectly sensible girl, but seated in a dining room or standing in a theatre queue she becomes Lady Croker of Bung Hall. I used to chide her gently about this prep-school attitude towards service people; tried to point out that nobody touches the forelock any more in this free and generous society of ours. After all, I said, the man who cuts Bert's grass every Wednesday morning may own a few shares of Gulf Canada too.

The waiter is a mean-looking devil with a head of rich coppery hair and a clever face—a sharp one for sure and nobody's fool. He listens to Molly, erect as a statue, his face a blank mask, the white napkin correctly folded across his sleeve. He is polite but is paying her little mind. She doesn't bother him. He made nearly ninety-five hundred last year and is good for a new Pontiac next spring, and in this country, when it comes right down to it, a man like that doesn't have to take any guff. When he withdraws he nods his head and smiles crisply but Molly is already frowning at the menu. She barely glances up when the maître d' pulls back the chair with an exquisite flourish and fusses over me as I am seated. I decide that for all his plainness of demeanour he is really a baroque character and right for the job. When he leaves, Molly looks up briefly to acknowledge my presence. There is a touch of affected boredom in her voice.

"Well, Wes, how have you been?"

"I'm fine, Molly. Sorry I'm late . . . An accident on the Parkway. It delayed everybody coming into town. . . ."

She is back to scanning the menu. "Don't worry about it . . . I just got here myself."

She reaches out without looking up and grasps her martini in slender fingers, taking it to her lips in one bold graceful motion. The glass just clears the corner of the menu. Molly has decided to punish me a little for being late. She is giving me the old silent treatment until I feel properly penitent. In the circumstances I could use a drink and cast about for the owner of new Pontiacs. He is nowhere to be seen. When Molly finally closes the menu, it is to prop her elbows on the table and hold her drink in both hands, looking over at me for the first time.

"Well, you don't look starved. You've been taking care of yourself, I see."

"Yes, I'm all right."

"You've put on weight."

"A pound or two, maybe, but I feel trim enough."

"Oh, come on now, Wes." She laughs. "More than a pound or two, surely. Your face is actually pudgy."

"Nonsense."

"It's true, my darling husband. You're getting fat."

"Oh, these are unkind words to a vain man."

She smiles and puts down her glass, running a finger around the rim. Her nails are painted scarlet and glow like bloodstones in the lamp light.

"So, you're still with Winchester House . . . What is it now? Nearly four months? That must be some kind of record. You better be careful, Wes, or people will start thinking you're getting serious about a few things. . . . And we couldn't have that, now, could we?"

I light her cigarette from the candle lamp, shielding the flame with my hand. She wants to know about the job and how I'm making out. She is like a school principal with a truant child: trying to gather an impression of my attitude before coming to any decision.

"The company has been sold, you know . . . to Universal Electronics . . ."

"The computer people?"

"Yes."

At this news Molly turns her head slightly and pushes out her lower lip, a gesture of her father's. It always suggests that she's impressed in spite of herself. Bert always accompanies it with some such expression as "Well, well" or "You don't say now."

"Janet Corby's husband works for them, I think . . . in accounting . . ."

"Is that a fact? And who's Janet Corby?"

Molly looks pained. "Oh don't be such a bore, Wes. You know perfectly well who Janet Corby is." She takes a deep drag on the cigarette. "And so where is all this going to leave little Winchester House?"

"Well, there will probably be quite a few changes over the next little while. This is just a guess . . ."

"Uh, huh . . . and what kind of changes?"

"Oh, there'll probably be more money pumped into the business. Universal will expand it. They'll diversify the line . . . more hardware . . ."

Molly leans back and lets her hands fall limp-wristed to her chest, another of her Southern belle stances. "My stars . . . will you just listen to the man talk? Why you sound like a real businessman, Wes."

"Don't I just, though? I amaze myself sometimes."

"You surely do amaze me, honey . . ."

"Anyway . . . there'll probably be staff changes, too. I think some people are going to get the axe."

"Oh! Like who, for instance?"

"Well . . . probably Syd Calhoun for one."

Molly smiles severely at this. "Well, now, that will be no great loss, will it . . . God what an oaf that man is."

"Oh, Syd has a few rough edges but he's a pretty good man."

"Nonsense. He's as crude as a sailor. Last summer he was always over at our cottage in his shorts. You could almost see his bloody jock strap . . ."

"Oh, Molly . . ." I have to laugh.

". . . smelling of perspiration and grinning like the village idiot. Always after you to play some silly croquet game or badminton. God, last summer he *discovered* badminton . . ."

"Well, Syd's an athletic guy . . ."

"If only he wouldn't stand so close and talk all over you . . ."

This is true. When Sydney is conversing he often finds it necessary to push his face right up into yours and talk lip to ear like a man selling watches on the street.

"I can't imagine he's much good at his job . . ."

"Well, as a matter of fact, he's very good at his job."

"And that of course explains why you think he's going to be sacked?"

"No . . . no, it doesn't . . . He'll be sacked for other reasons . . . wrong style . . ."

"And where is all this going to leave our wandering boy?"

"You mean me, of course?"

"Who else?"

I take a deep breath and lean forward, splayed across the table with my elbows out like a drunk with his story. "I will tell you, Molly, that I honestly believe my stock is rather high at the moment . . ."

Molly smiles suspiciously. "Oh sure, and what makes you think so?"

She takes up her glass by the stem and rotates it slowly like a jeweller. "What makes you think you won't get the axe too, Mister?"

"Oh, I don't know . . . just a feeling . . . I brought this manuscript in, you see, and right now . . ."

"Yes, I know about that."

She looks away, studying our closest neighbours. The girl loves to startle me.

"How do you know?" I ask.

"Your friend Calhoun phoned Daddy tonight. In a fit of Christmas spirit, I suppose. He was in his cups. He fawns all over Daddy, as you know . . ."

"Yes."

"Well, they talked about you. Calhoun thinks you've got a very bright future. He thinks you're a little lazy but definitely bright. . . . There now. How do you like that?"

"Oh, bless his good heart!"

"He told Daddy about this book."

"The book was sheer luck, you understand. An old school acquaintance . . ."

"What difference does it make? Calhoun said something about the president and you. You were standing arm in arm . . ."

"Oh, indeed. Harry and I are old pals . . ."

"Well, I don't see why you should be so self-effacing. For goodness' sake, Wes, if you're doing your job properly, why not be proud of it? Why make a silly joke out of everything?"

"Well . . ."

"I suppose you'd much rather be grubbing around in the ground with your Japanese landscaping friend . . ."

"No. My Japanese landscaping friend is in Florida right now, but he'll be back in the spring to grub around in the ground again . . ."

"And you'll be with him?" Molly looks hard at me.

"I don't know. I doubt it."

"Why?" She cracks out the question like a police captain.

"I'm reasonably satisfied with what I'm doing right now."

Molly looks away again.

"You know I spent an afternoon this week in Bill Loomis's office?"

"Oh yes. And how's old Bill?"

Bill Loomis is a bachelor lawyer and an old family friend: a big bear-like man who looks enough like Bert Sinclair to pass for his brother. When I worked at the Boulder Corporation I was told that there is no finer probate lawyer in Canada. I also heard he is a swordsman of some repute and has in fact bedded some of the wealthiest widows in the country. He used to turn up now and then for Sunday dinner at the Sinclairs'. He would tell discreet funny stories about the wills of eccentric trust-company presidents and investment brokers, sometimes using dialect and slicing the air with his large hands like a comedian on *Ed Sullivan*, the huge onyx cuff-links and signet rings flashing around like dark eyes. We never took to each other and he never really approved of me or the marriage. "He flatly advised me to get a divorce. Said he would arrange everything. He thinks you're a hopeless case."

"And I think he's a pompous old shit."

"Oh, don't be childish. Bill has only my best interests at heart."

"Was he looking up your dress all the time?"

"Well, you can still be as disgusting as ever, can't you?"

The waiter stands over us, his bookmaker's face small

and full of sly street-corner wisdom beneath the flaming hair. He is sizing me up, figuring out what I do for a living and how much I make. I have noticed that waiters and taxi drivers pride themselves on this ability to size people up. This one spends many hours standing in the passageway near the kitchen telling the younger waiters how he does it. His name is Bruno, according to the plastic nameplate on his tight-fitting vermilion jacket. I ask Bruno to bring us big drinks while Molly busies herself lining up knife, fork, and spoons all in a row, taking great pains to be orderly and precise. For a while we both watch her hands work, looking on with the same absent sidelong gaze one might reserve for a stranger's chess game in the park. I can sense a gathering of forces in the air and am not surprised when Molly folds her hands before her and fixes me with a grave look. When she speaks, her voice is low and charged with feeling, but she is determined to keep control and avoid the old dissolving scenes.

"Wes . . . I want to know this. Are you really interested in keeping the three of us together?"

"Of course."

"You want this marriage to go on?"

"Yes. You know that, Molly."

"Do I, though? Jesus!"

She unfolds her hands and leans in on her elbows. "Excuse me, but I just don't understand. You say you want our marriage to continue, and yet for the past five years . . ."

She looks away and takes up with the knives and spoons again, settling each in its place, carefully smoothing out the tablecloth. "Don't you think it's time you settled a few things?"

"Yes. Probably."

"All this drifting about. I'm fed up. I mean this, Wes.

I'm fed up to here and I simply refuse to put up with it any longer. If that makes me sound like a nagging bitch, too bad . . ."

"You mustn't expect too much from me, Molly. I've told you this before."

"Expect too much?"

She lifts her head and looks at me askance. "Now, that's a funny way of putting it. I suppose that asking you to hold on to a job for longer than a few months is expecting too much?"

"No, I don't mean that . . . I mean the success thing."

"Oh, the success thing, I see . . ." She leans forward and laughs roughly like an old actress.

"God, you can be a phony, Wes . . . the old success thing . . . what a lot of crap! Yes, I'll say it . . . our brave young hero does not wish to be corrupted by success. He is above all that, a proud and poor man . . . not for him the seats of the mighty and powerful. Oh, come off it, Wes. I've heard that one too many times before. This pose of yours is get-ing a little tiresome."

Molly believes that the only reason I am not successful is because I am wilfully opposed to worldly success. In her eyes I am a thwarted idealist who has difficulty coming to terms with life as it is lived in our day and age. This is not so. I am not opposed to worldly success and am no more a thwarted idealist than a pygmy's uncle. The truth is that I am not a success because I cannot think straight for days on end, bemused as I am by the weird trance of this life and the invisible passage of time. Molly's voice is taking on new strength and I pay heed, listening to every word, as watchful as a jay.

"But there will have to be changes, Wes!"

"Changes?" I perk up my head.

"Yes. In the first place, we're going to have to find a new apartment."

"I have a lease."

"Well, leases can be broken. Your place is too small, you know that yourself. We'll need at least a large two-bedroom, and here in the city handy to the school. I know you're close to your work now, but sunk in that godforsaken suburb of yours . . . I couldn't face that. We'll look for a flat in an older house downtown, along one of the quiet streets. Perhaps near Craigleigh Gardens or some place like that. Daddy is perfectly willing to help us out until we get organized. He knows that school isn't cheap. Look, Wes . . . we can make all this work if you really want to, but it has to be the absolute last chance for us. Can you see that?"

"Yes, I can see that, Molly."

"I've been making some plans." She scratches at the water goblet with a fingernail. "The first thing is this. I'd like to enroll Andrew as a day pupil at the school. We can drop him off in the morning and pick him up in the evening. This way he'll get the professional help he needs during the day and still enjoy the benefits of a home life. I've talked to Dr. Fortescue about it and he seems to think it's a good idea, at least for a while. They advised me to give it a two- or three-months trial. The second thing is that I'm going back to work."

"Do you think you're strong enough for that? What does Dr. Gault say?"

Molly quickly lights another cigarette, snapping out the match and sending forth a tremendous cloud of smoke through her pursed lips. "I haven't seen Gault for weeks. I gave all that up."

The smoke gathers in upon the candle lamp, shivering the flame and roiling upward in a grey-blue funnel.

"I just lost my faith in psychoanalysis, that's all. All that stuff about bed-wetting and girlhood chums . . . shit . . . I just don't believe it anymore. It's like religious faith. When you lose it, you lose it. It's gone and nothing can bring it back. Anyway, I'm sleeping better now. And I can't see how the job is going to hurt me. In fact, I can see it doing me a lot of good."

"I agree . . . What's the job?"

"Well, listen . . . It's funny . . ."

For a moment Molly lapses into the old easy ways of address. We might be back on an old date talking about each other's day. Then she swiftly checks herself. Although she wants the stamp of my approval on her plans, Molly relishes this distance between us and the high ground she now occupies.

"The other day I met an old professor of mine, Cyril Hamilton. In the Colonnade book shop. He's just been given the headship of his department and he was looking for a secretary. He asked me what I was doing these days and the first thing I know he offered me the job. Well, after all, I did major in his damn subject and so I should know something about what's going on. Actually, he told me there isn't all that much to do but he wants someone he can depend on and someone who knows a little bit about university life. So . . . I'm going to start in the new term and I don't mind saying I'm rather excited by it all."

"Well, I think you should be. It sounds good to me."

"Does it really?"

She looks at me over the cigarette smoke, squinty-eyed and wary. ". . . or is that just another of your glib expressions . . . God, I hope not . . ."

Suddenly she is overtaken by aggressive high spirits. The brimming rich promise of things is too much for her nature and it beckons after release. She crushes out her cigarette violently and leans in towards me.

"Damn it all, Wes . . . for the first time in months I feel really confident about things. At last a few things are starting to jell. You've found a decent job and one that doesn't appear to bore you completely to death. And I would make a guess here, too."

"What's that?"

She pokes about in the ashtray with her matchbox, tamping down the smouldering cigarette. "Oh . . . only this . . . that you're doing better at your job than you care to admit."

"Well, perhaps . . ."

"Anyway—I just feel confident, that's all."

"Well, good—so do I, then."

"You don't have to say that if you don't mean it."

"I mean it."

Our dinner is a success, I think. I order a bottle of Chianti and call upon the gods of good cheer to wait upon our table. The food is as good as I remember it and the accordion player's in his prime, singing Christmas songs from the old country. He is a sight in his wide-sleeved satin shirt open at the throat. With his dark curly hair and stiff moustaches he looks for all the world like the man who sells Gallo corn oil on television. Bruno is in a temper and ministers unto us with a sulky look, his ginger brow knitted in irritation. I humour him, however, with a show of courtesy bordering on the downright meek.

Forking succulent lasagna into my mouth, I listen to Molly tell me about her yoga lessons and how they are helping her to sleep at night. It is all a matter of natural relaxation, according to her teacher, Rama Gupta. Molly is elated telling me all this, but I confess to being touched by a mild sadness. This yoga business is another of her very special diversions and it will lead her down the same path. On some noncommittal Tuesday in February she will cast it aside and then we will all be in for a bad time. It will go the way of the French lessons and the folk singing and the volunteer work for retarded children.

Oh, but my Molly is full of plans tonight and there is nothing to do but sit in this pleasant place and cover her hands with mine. How beautiful she is in her excellent suit and swanky hairdo! Like a good American wife, she is already planning dinners for Harry Ingram and the boys from Universal. What fine dinners they will be, too! I am forced to think of Ron Tuttle, the poor bastard. He and his mousy little woman don't really stand a chance.

On the way out Molly squeezes my hand like a lover and tells me she is sorry about the Holocaust bottle.

"I knew you had it around for a long time, but I had no idea it held any significance. God, I'm really sorry, Wes."

"It's all right. I was overwrought that day."

"And how Ernie and I laughed. And it wasn't all that funny, was it?"

"No, but it's over now and you musn't worry about it."

In the parking lot across the street from Martino's I stand, bent over, with my hands along the roof of Molly's car. Large wet snowflakes settle and melt on the back of my neck. The little car idles with its deep thrumming sound and fills the air with a gassy smell. I watch Molly's gloved fingers drum upon the black steering wheel.

"Won't you come back to the apartment for a nightcap?"

"No, I can't."

"Why not?"

"I have to see some people."

"Are you going to a party now?"

The drumming stops.

"It's at the Houghs'. Their annual Christmas do. I couldn't refuse or Ernestine would never forgive me . . . I'm only going to stop by for a drink . . . look at me . . . I'm not dressed for a party . . ."

"How about taking me?"

"Now listen, Wes . . . let's not rush things along. This has been a good evening so far . . . Let's just take it slowly."

"Okay, but I'd enjoy another drink with you."

"I know, but I need to take everything nice and easy this time. I don't intend to go dashing madly here and there. This has been a good start."

"All right."

"You're still coming to dinner on Sunday? I'll be counting on that, so don't disappoint me at the last moment."

"No, I'll be there."

"Come around four and we'll have time for drinks."

"All right."

"Daddy really has the place looking festive. I think you'll enjoy yourself. . . . Well, I better go now."

"Take it easy, Molly."

"Yes . . . you too."

She spins away and the little car jumps down the ramp and into the street traffic, its brake-lights blinking like hot red eyes in the snow.

7.

The snow does not amount to much and soon gives way to a mild night in which the clouds hang low. The downtown sky glows lurid and feverish like some antique painting of the Great London Fire. The air is sooty and damp as mildew. I can hear water dripping as the snow melts on the balcony railings above me. When the telephone rings, I am sure it is Molly calling from an upstairs bedroom at the Houghs', asking me to come fetch her. But it is Helen Corbett and her voice is scratchy as an old record. She is uneasy about things. For that matter, we are both embarrassed and conversation is difficult, even painful. We converse with each other like strangers on a bus.

"Well, I'm sure you must be looking forward to the holidays."

"Yes, I am. I feel I really need a rest."

"I can imagine . . . Where are you calling from, Helen?"

"Oh, I'm at the apartment. Actually I'm ready to leave, all packed. I'm driving home tonight."

"Home?"

"Yes, to Harrisville to my parents."

"Oh, I see . . . You're going tonight?"

"Yes, I am. I've been trying to reach you for quite a while."

"Well, I was out to dinner. I just came in the door."

"I hope . . . you had dinner with your wife."

"Well, yes, I did."

"I'm glad, really I am. I know it's none of my business, but I'm glad."

"Thank you."

"Wes . . . I want to tell you something. I know it sounds crazy but I couldn't leave for home until I told you . . . I've been sitting by this phone since seven o'clock."

"God, what's wrong?"

"Oh, nothing's wrong exactly . . . It's just that I want you to know that last night . . . what happened, I mean."

"What happened?"

"Yes, you know . . . what I did."

"Ah, yes . . . that."

"Yes . . . that . . . I had an awful lot to drink. Well, I just want you to know that I don't do that every night . . . with everybody . . ."

"I know you don't, Helen."

"I don't know what you must think of me."

Somewhere a siren howls and I can see the traffic below

stop at the intersection of Union and Napier to await the emergency vehicle. What do I think of her? Yes.

"Listen, Helen . . . I'm going to tell you something now and I want you to listen carefully. All right?"

"Yes?"

"What you did last night . . ."

The yellow police car speeds westward, its rotating roof light flashing red.

". . . was an honest act of affection . . ."

The police car shoots through the intersection like a burning arrow and disappears behind the grey sides of the apartment buildings, its howl rising and falling away against the brick and cement.

". . . God knows, honesty is rare enough anymore . . . I just won't have you feeling bad about something that was open and . . . decent. Are you listening to me?"

I am as stern as a drill sergeant with her.

"Yes."

"Just remember this, Helen, please. What we did last night . . . was private . . . between you and me. . . . Now I'll tell you what I want you to do. All right?"

"Yes? What?" Her voice is as small as a child's.

"I want you to go up to Harrisville with this thought in your mind . . . that I think you're a very fine person."

"Oh, damn it all, Wes . . . sometimes I'm so confused . . . about things."

"I know how you feel, believe me."

Suddenly I am overcome by fatigue, flattened right out by a massive numbing tiredness. My arms feel as heavy as planks. My head droops forward on my neck. Helen tells me that I am warm and understanding but I am also a married man. She does not want to complicate her life.

"I don't think we should see each other again."

I am silent, holding the telephone now in both hands.

"It's nothing against you. I like you as a person but I think it would be best all round if we stopped seeing each other."

It is an effort to open my mouth. "You're probably right, but I want you to remember what I said."

"I will, Wes, and thank you."

"You're welcome."

"I want to wish you every success in your marriage."

"Thank you very much."

"Good-bye, Wes."

"Good-bye, Helen."

It is all I can do to drag myself to the basket chair, there to sit with a large whisky, the last of the Holocaust bottle. Helen Corbett is now hurrying down the hallway of a building called The Diplomat, her chalk-white bottle-shaped body wrapped up in high boots and a Doctor Zhivago coat. Taking the elevator to the underground parking lot and her stout little Valiant. In ten minutes she will be hissing along the Macdonald-Cartier Freeway, nodding her dark head to the radio music. Mom and Dad are waiting up, drinking Instant Sanka. They think she's been on a big date with that very special guy. Jesus!

In bed I draw the sheets to my chin and listen to my neighbour's television: a late-night talk show from New York. The host and his two guests are talking about their childhood Christmases. One of the guests is a famous actress. In the forties and early fifties she was something of a sex-pot. Then she married a Nevada businessman and dropped from public view, only to reappear as the heroine of a situation comedy series in which she played the wife of a stupid but good-natured businessman. She was brought up in a small town in Wisconsin, one of eight children. Her father was a brakeman on the railroad.

"We were poor, believe you me." She laughs a little at the memory of this poverty. "When I think of the gifts my children get today. In those days we were lucky if we got a pair of woollen mittens or a good warm scarf. Still, you know—it wasn't the gifts that really mattered then. It was —oh, I don't know—a feeling—just being all together and walking out to church on Christmas morning. And the Christmas dinner. Oh, that dinner!"

Now the famous actress describes *that* dinner with her brakeman father standing to say grace before carving the turkey. Then there was her first Christmas away from home. She was a young actress in New York, friendless and broke. She can remember phoning her folks collect on Christmas Eve and that was the first time she heard her father weep. She tells all this in her low agreeable voice. The host is a pleasant man but excitable. He sounds very excited about all this. He really can't get over how beautiful it was.

"It was all so simple and beautiful then, wasn't it?" he says. "Yes, it was," the famous actress says.

The other guest is a famous novelist. He is not so famous as the actress, but neither is he unknown to thousands. I myself read one of his novels years ago—a best-seller about a young man torn between the priesthood and the woman he loved. I can't remember what he decided to do but I can remember the author's "picturesque" style. He could really set a scene, and listening to him now I am reminded of this. It seems that he too was brought up in a small town, in New England. He can remember walking to midnight mass through the softly falling snow, listening to the peal of chapel bells and the glad cries of the worshippers. This works up the host again and he keeps breaking in to say, "That's beautiful, Bill, really beautiful. You know—I think what we're talking about here is really something quite beautiful and quite sad. And maybe a lot of you people out there who are over thirty will get this feeling too. I think what we're really talking about here is a beautiful vanishing thing in American life . . ."

He is very excited. It is all too much for him and he can't work it out. I think he would like to cry.

THE WEEKEND MAN
IV

1.

This morning I awakened to a state of fierce exaltation. I recognize the state for what it is—the soaring Saturday-morning state of readiness and expectation—and I am on my guard, moving around like a crab in strange waters, my feelers casting about suspiciously. At times like this, one must watch for disaster or at the very least bad news.

Next to Friday afternoon, however, Saturday morning is the best time of the week. I have always believed this and now it has been confirmed in the finest American tradition of public-opinion polls. I read about it in the Life and Leisure column of *Newsweek* magazine. Or it could have been *Time*. The Life and Leisure column lets me in on what my fellow North Americans are thinking and doing these days. According to this recent poll, seventy-two per cent of them think Saturday morning between nine and eleven is the best time of the week. On the other hand, eighty-eight per cent agree that Sunday night between eleven and twelve is the worst time of all.

In my exalted state, then—buoyed up by readiness and expectation—I am vigilant and do what I usually do in this condition. I sit down and make a list of things that need doing. This morning's list looks like this:

1. Destroy the slips of paper in the peanut butter jars.
2. Have breakfast. Whatever comes first into head.
3. Phone brother Frank.
4. Straighten apartment.
5. Phone Harold Pendle about ms.
6. Christmas shopping.

After emptying the peanut butter jars into the garbage, I eat a slice of lemon jelly roll and brew a pot of By Appointment to Her Majesty Tea, using the last bag from a package of Earl Grey left behind by Molly. Seated on the arm of the sofa, I submit to an impulse and switch on the television for a little company. It is A.M. *Playhouse* and they are showing the movie of Dickens's *Christmas Carol*. Old Alistair Sim plays Scrooge and he has just awakened to discover that it's Christmas morning. This puts *him* into an exalted state, but he has no mind to be cautious. He is incontrovertibly committed to mirth, and capers around his rooms like a madman, waving his skinny arms. *Whoops, halloo there. They've done it, bless them. They've done it and all in one night.* He sinks to his knees in a swoon and embraces the bedpost. *Oh, Jacob, dear Jacob. Oh, spirits. I swear. I swear.*

I'll be a better man, I swear it. Oh, whoops. Halloo . . .

Leaning forward, I spread my fingers across my kneecaps and watch Scrooge move through the streets of old London, calling to this one and that one, pressing a coin into a blind man's hand here, patting the head of an urchin there. He is in a rare humour. I know the feeling. When I was twelve years old an evangelist named Sunny Hill came to Middlesburgh and he put *me* in a rare humour one night in the Evangel Hall. He was a husky young man, a Southerner with curly brown hair and a face pitted by acne. Once upon a time he had been a prizefighter, a fact which impressed me mightily. He stood at the front of the hall and waved a Bible at me.

"Ah used to faght men fer a livin'," he cried. "Yas and ah did mah fayer share o' sinnin' too, friends. But then ah heard mah Saviour callin' and naow ah'm ony innerested in knockin' out the devil, and not with these either." He held up two huge fists and shook them at me. "No suh, with this," he shouted, holding up the Bible again. Then he grinned. "Though mind you, if that old devil gits frisky and wants to come out and faght like a man, ah won't be 'fraid to give hem a few licks." Then he slipped under an invisible punch and flicked a few quick jabs in the air. When the piano began to play "Jesus Is Calling You," I walked to the front of the hall and stood looking up at Sunny Hill's glistening pockmarked face, beside myself with joy. I wonder what that bird is up to these days. Anyway, for a week or so, I was just like the reformed Scrooge, walking around in a rapture, smiling at people and looking for ways to be kind and good. The only trouble was that sooner or later I had to come back down to earth. Now, looking at old Scrooge huffling along there giving away his money, I am forced to think of the day when he comes back down to earth and no longer feels so excellent about things. Pondering this makes me lean forward at a sharp angle. With my fingers drumming against my kneecaps I find myself frowning ever so slightly at A.M. *Playhouse*. The danger here is that I could lose my good humour altogether. In the circumstances it is best to turn off the television and phone Middlesburgh. Kitty answers, out of breath, running from some corner of my father's big house.

"Ohhh . . . hello . . ."

"Hi, Kitty. It's Wes."

"Wes!" She is delighted. "Honey, how are you?"

"Fine, Kit . . . and you?"

"Couldn't be . . . better . . . ohhh, let me get my breath . . . I was in the basement."

She laughs. It is easy for me to picture her standing by the kitchen telephone with a flushed cheek, fanning herself with a tea towel.

"Well, it's good to hear from *you*. Are you coming up?"

"Uh, no, I'm not, actually . . . I'm really sorry. I should have phoned earlier . . ."

"Well, that's okay, but where are you going? You're not going to be alone?"

"No, no, I'm going to be with Molly. At her parents."

"Uh huh . . . and how is Molly?" She says this quickly. It is an obstacle to get by.

"She's fine. Really in good spirits these days."

"Wonderful. And you sound happy too."

"Well, I am. I feel good."

"I'm so glad, Wes. We worry about you, you know. But we are sorry we won't see you. Frank will be so disappointed. We all will be. The kids . . ."

"Well . . ."

"We have presents here for you."

"Oh, Kit . . ."

"I guess you'd like to talk to Frank but gee you've missed him. He's at the Arena. Saturday morning, you know, and Donny's playing a big game. They all seem to be big games these days, real life-and-death struggles to hear him talk."

We both laugh.

"I just know Frank is going to be sorry he missed you."

There is real anxiety in Kitty's tone. She has always believed that there is something special between Frank and me. When she would see us together with Frank kneading my shoulder and me jollying him along, she would beam at us like a favourite aunt as though to say: What a wonderful thing you two have going for you. Kitty was an only child.

"Well, I should have known Frank would be at the rink this morning. It was stupid of me. Look . . . wish him a Merry Christmas for me, and the kids too, of course."

"Oh, Wes, I will . . . and when are you going to come and see us?"

"Well, sometime in the new year for sure, Kit. Real soon. We'll take a whole weekend. Molly loves to ski, you know."

"Oh, yes?"

Kitty is trying to puzzle this through. Have Molly and I decided to try again? Are we living together now? It is exciting but she is too polite to ask and I am not up to explaining things.

"So take care, Kit, and we'll be seeing you, eh!"

"Oh sure, Wes, and thanks so much for calling. I'm so sorry you missed Frank."

"Yes. Well, it couldn't be helped. My fault. I'll be talking to you again soon now."

"Right, Wes. Bye."

"Bye, bye."

It will occur to Kitty at about the time she hangs the receiver back on the hook that she forgot to ask about Andrew. This will probably ruin her day.

I call Harold Pendle's number and speak to one of his leggy long-haired daughters. Her name is Sheila and she sounds clever and grown-up.

"Mommy and Daddy aren't here now. May I take a message?"

She must be watching A.M. *Playhouse* too. I can hear Scrooge cackling away as he frightens the wits out of poor Bob Cratchit by announcing a salary increase. I strain to listen.

"Not there . . . I see . . ."

"No . . . they are curling this morning."

"Oh . . . well, fine. I wonder, Sheila, if you would mind telling your daddy that Mr. Wakeham called."

"Mr. Wakeham? Yes, sir."

"Thank you, Sheila."

"You're welcome, sir."

The low-pressure front has passed in the night and a sharp blast of arctic air has moved across southern Ontario to scour the sky a deep blue. It is a fine nippy day, but Union Place looks somehow vulnerable and raw this morning with her long grey streets stretched out under the cold sunlight. In the Shopping Plaza parking lot the roofs of the cars glitter with a quick metallic brilliance. I stand on my balcony and watch the Tom Thumb Traffic Helicopter dip low to the southwest and then climb, making the skittering sideways motion of a dragonfly as it spins northward out over the valley and the Parkway. It reminds me that I should take the Dart in for a check-up, though right now I prefer to stand here and look at the two CPA stewardesses on the balcony of a neighbouring apartment. They are stringing

Christmas lights along the railing, going about it with the same calculated poise and efficiency they might call on when serving sixty chicken dinners twenty thousand feet above the earth. This business of setting up lights is supposed to be a man's job but there is certainly no female botching going on here. These girls know what they're about and they work well together, unravelling the cords and screwing in the coloured bulbs, looking capable and dexterous in their snug-fitting jeans and suede jackets. It is a pleasure to watch them.

These stewardesses moved into Union Terrace a week or so after Molly left. They took a one-bedroom unit down the hall from me. I like the looks of one of them; she's a cute friendly little human with short chestnut hair and a chunky arm, the sort of girl that should answer to Cathy or Deb. I met her, too. It was just like one of those movies about New York where the fellow meets the girl in the elevator and she's overburdened with parcels and one bag is already bursting. Obviously she's in difficulty and this fellow takes the parcels in his good strong arms and carries them up to her apartment. She sets about making coffee, inviting him to have a cup, and first off they discover they have all sorts of things in common. This happened to me or some of it. I helped the little stewardess with her parcels all right—took them straight through to the galley (as she called it) and put them down on the arborite counter. She peeled away the jacket of her uniform and smiled the warmest of smiles while I grinned my very best grin. But it was clear as daylight she had no intention of making coffee or asking me to stay to chat. I left, a thanked and helpful stranger. Now, when we meet in the hall or in the laundry room, she always says hello and gives me the warmest of smiles. I know men who would interpret these smiles as an invitation to get better acquainted but I am not fooled. My little stewardess is giving me the smiles that girls reserve for pals and older brothers. Somehow she has contrived to see me as a polite acquaintance, the man to call on in emergencies.

Now she's spotted me and waves, leaning over the railing like a ship's passenger. Her roommate is a medium-size blonde with a bored pretty face. She looks across too and right through me to a point behind my head. I am as invisible to her as the balcony I stand on—just another pleasant indefinite North American male face. She has seen thousands of us and it is going to take an unusual set of features to hold her gaze. Now my little stewardess smiles her warmest smile. Hi there, it says. I grin back, giving her my Oliver Hardy wave, holding up my hand claw-like at the shoulder level, my fingers playing an imaginary keyboard.

2.

The Shopping Plaza is thronged with people today. In the Arcade Department Store we graze one another and sidle along from counter to counter, inspecting this and rejecting that. The fabulous prodigal variety of it all! It never fails to amaze me, though I am a poor shopper and am likely to wander down the wide aisles as abstracted as a visitor from one of the Iron Curtain countries.

In the jewellery department I watch a middle-aged man examine a wrist watch. He is a pleasant-looking fellow in his beige car coat and dinky high-crowned fedora. The fedora gives him a youthful air. The smoke from his pipe is spiced and aromatic and drifts under my nose with a rich pleasing fragrance, a silent herald of his pleasantness. He does not remove the pipe from his mouth but puffs it meditatively, cocking his head to one side as he turns the watch over and over, looping his hand through the expansion bracelet to check its tension—a thoughtful consumer of life's goods. The clerk is a young man, a college student working the holidays. He leans across the glass counter on his forearms, swivelling his head around to watch me, a studied look of boredom on his apple-cheeked face. This look shoots out a message to me. The message says this is not a permanent job. Actually I attend university and will be a management consultant one day. It is not the young clerk, however, who interests me. What I would really like to do is to tap the pleasant-looking man on the shoulder and ask him to consider that he stands in a market place no ancient emperor or Renaissance prince could have imagined to exist. And, considering this, does it not give him pause? But of course I do no such thing. That is a good way to involve the authorities in your life.

In sporting goods I espy a familiar face. It is none other than Billy Goat Bellamy, the lecherous high-school chemist of Union Place, standing now dapper and trim in tweed cap, scarf, and belted sports coat. With a pair of plus-fours he could easily pass for a vintage British golfer. Only now he is Bellamy, the practised angler testing the weight and feel of a fly rod as he snaps it back and forth with a supple wrist. He is waiting for the clerk to finish with another customer and, like many persons who find themselves alone in public places, he does not wish to appear ill at ease. Thus he is the picture of nonchalance, standing there flicking the fly rod, not about to be rushed for anything. If I were to step up to him now and announce that his coattails were on fire, he would only give me an ironic look and say, "Is that a fact now. Well, well, so they are. What a damn nuisance!" And then set about brushing away the flames in an unhurried fashion. It is a carefully arrived-at posture and has probably taken years to perfect. When the customer finally leaves, Bellamy returns the fly rod to the rack and takes his purchase to the clerk. It's a mechanical hockey game for youngsters. As the clerk wraps it up, Bellamy picks a canister of tennis balls from the counter and gives it a good shake, arching his eyebrows with a glance that says: Now *these* are what I call tennis balls. When he departs he trails one hand along the counter, absently exploring the merchandise. As he gets beyond sporting goods he hefts the hockey game under one arm and accelerates, moving off quickly through the crowd with his peculiar little spinning stride.

My Christmas shopping goes well this year. In an hour I am standing in the raw sunlight in front of Woolworth's eating a Mars bar. Between my legs is a snow-white bag with Santa's face on both sides. In the bag are a Mexican stone necklace for Molly, an English teddy bear for Andrew (who has a great passion for bears, already owning several but always willing to make room for a newcomer), a large colourful book entitled *New Ways to Better Flower Arrangement*, my peace offering to Mildred. And, for Bert, an imported briar and a pound tin of Bond Street. Seventy-six dollars and fourteen cents including tax—a small enough price to pay for goodwill in these times.

Behind my dark glasses I study an older couple who stand waiting at the bus stop. What is it in their faces that I see? They're retired and have probably come in from Melody Court, the senior citizens' home out at Trexflen and Belvedere. They are both carrying Santa Claus bags like mine. She's large and shapeless with a puffy face and slack arthritic limbs. She stares around with ill humour from behind her rimless glasses. The man is lean as a hoe with a wattled neck and darting blue eyes: a checkerboard politician for sure, and away from her a man of opinions. I saw them not ten minutes ago in the stationery department. She was choosing an anniversary card for her daughter, making her selection with a ponderous scrutiny, turning the cards over in her plump fingers to read the verses with slowly moving lips. Now they stand looking about the Plaza with their severe country frown, saying not a word. They might be total strangers for all the attention they afford one another. When the bus arrives she climbs aboard to settle heavily into the window seat, the Santa Claus bag resting in her lap. He puts his bag between his legs and sits upright, his neck stretched out like a turkey and his arms folded across his chest. As the bus pulls away the woman turns her face to the window to gaze at the passing scene and I think I perceive what it is. Yes, there is no question about it now. It is hatred I see.

3.

In front of the Brewers' Retail I stand listening to "Jingle Bells" on the loudspeaker, looking out over the parking lot and across the street to the apartment buildings. Union Terrace is a tall white rectangle and dissects the blue sky in neat geometric lines. Looking up, I spot one of the stewardesses stepping out onto her balcony to reconnoitre. This is a usual practice with people who live in apartment buildings like Union Terrace. We are always stepping out onto our balconies to reconnoitre. At any hour of the day or night you will find us doing this. Some, like myself, even have telescopes.

4.

Saturday afternoons are not so bad. Mine are usually given over to sports events on TV. Truly, on this the choicest of days, you will find me as sluggish as the veriest cartoon husband, sipping beer in my basket chair and watching golf matches from Bermuda or football games from Denver. It is a matter for some reflection, this Saturday afternoonness of mine. I am not unhappy, but the exaltation has definitely gone, levelled right into a torpor too flat for words. Thus sunk, I pass away the hours.

Today I watch a college basketball game from somewhere in the States, Ohio I think. The players are all lean in the shank and tall as Zulu warriors. They go racing up and down the court sinking a basket each time. The score has reached some astronomical figure. I'm not really that interested in the game and in a manner of speaking keep only one sleepy eye on it. The other eye is on the weekend paper where I am almost always drawn to the thrust and parry on the editorial page. Somebody named James J. Brown fairly smokes with wrathful indignation. It is not difficult to imagine this fellow sitting down to write his letter with a burning face. *Sir: I would like to know what Mr. Simon Blumenthal (Letter 19/12/ Victims of Our Own Technology) would have us do. Would Mr. Blumenthal really like us to turn the clock back and live a "simple existence" in his imagined golden age, unencumbered by his "chains of progress." I suggest he go to South Africa where I spent many years and visit the hut of a Hottentot: see what hunger is really like. I think it might change his tune in a hurry.* Mr. Brown has a point. It is much better to sit here and sip beer and watch a basketball game on television than to starve in the Kalahari. On the other hand, there is probably something to be said for Mr. Blumenthal and his "chains of progress." It is all extremely difficult and I know how these gentlemen feel. There was a time when I sat down to compose letters to the editor; little masterpieces of invective and sarcasm they were too. The outrage could last for days!

On my screen a young giant palms the ball like a peach and sends it spinning in the air. It drops through the basket without touching the rim. The crowd goes a little crazy and the cheerleaders, three white and two black girls, run out and leap in the air, cute little tricks all in their mini-skirts and ankle socks.

I open another beer and stretched out on my sofa read of an old friend named Joel Brewer. There is his name sure enough, in a column entitled What People Are Doing. It seems that Joel and his wife Heather and her parents Dr. and Mrs. Gordon Craig are spending the Christmas holidays in the Bahamas. Molly will be sure to notice this and suggest I ring up Joel in the new year and invite Heather and him for drinks some night. She will see their names in today's paper as a favourable omen. At last, things are falling into their rightful place. Inviting the Brewers for drinks will be seen as a natural progression in her new-start programme. It is the easiest thing to call Joel. I know he will be delighted to hear from me, though we haven't seen each other now for nearly three years.

Joel Brewer was best man at my wedding and once, standing at the bar like gentlemen in the basement of Delta Epsilon House, he told me I was the most honest person he'd ever met and he counted it a rare privilege to know me. Needless to say, I returned the compliment and we swore everlasting comradeship. We were a strange pair at university. Joel's parents were wealthy and he was something of a hotshot fraternity type, what some people in those days called a Big Man on Campus. He could play the part, too, with his shambling jowly handsomeness and that air of innocence and arrogance you often find in privately educated young men. As for myself, I was the classroom wit, the deliverer of cynical cracks from the rear of the lecture hall—a dubious stature, to be sure, but one Joel admired, disproportionately I always thought. I know he found me a strange character but he was fond of me and fussed over me a great deal. It bothered him, for instance, that I had no other real friends. Joel believed that a man should have a lot of friends and he was forever taking me around to Delta Epsilon House and introducing me to football players and future barristers, huge hearty fellows who drank a terrific amount of beer and brought along their big strapping St. Helen's girls to the Friday-night parties. Since I seldom had ten words to say to any of these people, no one remembered me from one day to the next and Joel would set about reintroducing me on another night.

Joel and I lost sight of each other after the wedding. The last time we talked was about three years ago on a downtown street during the noon hour. I recall that we were both in a hurry but we still clove to each other with all the old terrifying camaraderie of lifelong fraternity pals. He was selling bonds for his father's office and I was planting seedlings for Mr. Kito. He couldn't get over my job and kept shaking his head from side to side, grinning down at me. "Listen, old buddy. This is fantastic. What are you up to, anyway? You writing a goddam book or something? I wouldn't put it past you, you know. What a character you turned out to be! I always said you were a weird bugger. You know I told Molly that on your wedding day. But listen, Christ. I want to hear about this greenhouse thing. You and I have got to get together soon. Ask Molly to give Heather a call." I said I would and we parted, clasping one another a final time like young Roman senators.

5.

Sometime in the night I awaken still flat on the sofa surrounded by the pages of my weekend paper. Figures on the television screen flicker ghostly blue across the darkened room. It is a midnight mass from one of the downtown churches. The bishop himself is celebrant; he stands before the people and gravely swings the thurible back and forth, sending puffs of incense into the air. He is a broadshouldered muscular man, as solidly put together as a side of beef. The mitre fits his temples like a helmet and the chasuble is snug across his wide chest. There is altogether a fine meaty Rotarian look to him. The only trouble is that he stands in the glare of the television lights and they directly strike his square-cut glasses and cover his eyes with an amazing naked brilliance. It makes him look faintly sinister and as I watch him in his extraordinary garments with his eyes glazed out I cannot help but think that there is something of the primeval wizard about him, some elemental vestige of hocus-pocus and legerdemain.

Once Molly thought of becoming a Catholic. It was another of her enthusiasms. She took to reading the works of people like Jacques Maritain and marked up paperbacks with excellent titles like *True Humanism* and *On the Use of Philosophy*. But I think she was really attracted by this serious matter of ritual. And sitting with her, hunched over in the vast gloom of St. Michael's, it *was* difficult not to believe that something important was taking place before my eyes.

Now, leaning forward on the arborite counter of my kitchenette, I eat the last of the jelly loaf and listen to the people chant their prayers. The apartment is filled with this strange medieval sound. But what is it that these people want, bent over with their foreheads resting on their arms? What do they pray for here in this Canadian city on a winter night two thousand years after the Great Event? Do they really expect to see the blinding face of God one day? Is it some perpetual state of grace they seek, an unending supply of the old elusive happiness? Or do they just want a little guidance in the managing of this lonely business of living a life? I am at a loss to imagine, but it does occur to me that I have managed my own life rather badly. All this musing on the mystery and the wonder has only set up a wild howling in the soul. My father was probably right. It is far more sensible to submit to the numbness of the daily passage. Still, the thought leaves me with a sweet sick dread and I dial Molly's number. She answers in that abrupt perfunctory tone of late-night telephone users: all set to scold a wrong-number caller.

"Yes?"

"Molly . . . it's Wes."

"Wes?" Her surprise startles me. "What's wrong?"

"Why, nothing . . . nothing's wrong . . ."

"Do you know what time it is?"

Molly is pleased to hear from me but I am not about to be let off without some mild rebuke and this delivered in her old sorority-house telephone voice: well, I must say Saturday afternoon is a fine time to ask for a date.

"You scared us to death."

"I'm sorry."

"You know what a telephone call this time of night is like?"

"Yes."

"Why didn't you call earlier? I called you."

"When?"

"About eight. Andrew wanted to say good night. Oh, Wes, where have you been?"

"Well, I'm sorry. I fell asleep . . . on the damn couch this afternoon."

"A man called here for you earlier. Just before dinner."

"What man?"

"That author friend of yours, Pendle?"

"Author?"

"Yes. Apparently he got our number from your boss Calhoun. He's returning your call. He's been trying to reach you all afternoon. Is it important?"

"Not very."

"He wonders if you'd mind calling him tomorrow."

"Tomorrow is Christmas Day."

"Well, I don't know. He seemed very nice about it. He

spoke highly of you and said you've been a big help to him."

"I've been a big help to him? The man's an idiot."

"Now, Wes. Let's not get all clever and cynical again."

"Yes. Right."

Below on Napier Avenue a motorcycle policeman pulls into the empty Gulf station and parks his machine in the shadows behind a picket fence. After a moment he walks out and stands by the edge of the pavement, his white helmet gleaming under the lights of the big Gulf oval. He begins to flag down the passing cars with his flashlight, looking for drinking drivers, no doubt. I rub my neck and try to concentrate. Molly has had a few drinks and is in good spirits. She is talking about Andrew and something they all watched on television tonight.

"The *Nutcracker*?"

"Yes, silly. The *Nutcracker Suite*. You know—Tchaikovsky!"

"Oh, yes!"

"Oh, he just loved it, Wes. The music and all those silly dancing animals. It was great fun. He sat on the couch beside Daddy and laughed and clapped his hands."

I prop myself against the window sill and watch the motorcycle policeman. He has just stopped a rakish little sports job and is bent low talking to the driver. Molly wishes there had been snow for Andrew this Christmas. I do too, and listening to her, I decide on a plan.

"How would you like to go up to Middlesburgh on Boxing Day? The three of us, I mean. We can leave right after breakfast and be back before dinner. I've been talking to Kitty and she says they have lots of snow up there."

Molly considers the idea. She is not keen on visiting Frank and Kitty, but she would like Andrew to see the snow.

"We'll put him on one of the kids' sleighs and pull him over to the park. There are some little hills and slopes. I used to go there when I was a boy. What do you think?"

"All right," she says finally, brightening. "It sounds like fun."

With her mind now made up, Molly forthwith sets the plan in motion, settling on departure time and clothing, asking about the temperature and weather forecast for the next forty-eight hours. She is good at this sort of detail, actually enjoys looking into it. She will make a fine secretary for Professor Hamilton. I answer her questions and watch the policeman wave on the sports car with his flashlight. And then, as I stand by the window talking to my wife, I feel it stealing over me. It is here in the apartment with me covering everything: the old familiar gloom, the baffling ordinary sadness of my own existence. It surrounds me like a germ gas. To breathe is an affliction requiring real courage. At this hour of the long night the only anodyne for such sadness is the diversion of sweet flesh itself. Thus hoping against hope, I hold my breath and ask Molly to come over.

"It's only twenty minutes by taxi . . . or I could come for you . . ."

"Oh, Wes! It's no good to come together like this. I've told you before . . ."

"Yes, I know," I say glumly.

"Oh, hell! Why did we settle on tomorrow anyway? You could as easily have come over tonight." She pauses, thinking hard, half-irritated by it all.

"Would you like to come over tonight?"

"Well . . ."

I have a vision of myself standing on Bert's doorstep at one o'clock in the morning clutching my Air Canada bag.

"No . . . I don't think so, Molly."

"But you'd like to see me come over there?"

"No . . . no, I guess not. You're right. It isn't fair."

"I'm not talking about fairness, Wes . . . can't you see that?"

"All right, yes, I see. Only don't lecture me, Molly, please. I'm not up to it right now . . ."

"Look, darling . . . I would like to come over, I really would. But I just don't think it solves anything in our relationship when we come together just for sex. There is more . . ."

In our relationship. Wonderful. Come together just for sex. Yes. Excellent. The policeman waves a large dark sedan into the service-station lot.

"Pardon?"

"I know you're lonely. So am I, but don't make it difficult . . ."

"I'll survive, Molly . . . So will you. We'll both survive . . ."

"Oh, don't be so damn flippant and listen for a minute. Why don't you come over tomorrow morning for breakfast? We'll wait for you and open the presents when you get here." She is excited by the idea. Of course, why didn't I think of this before?"

"All right."

"Will you do that?"

"Yes."

"Good. I'll make an omelette for you and some coffee and we'll watch Andrew open his gifts."

"Excellent."

"Oh, darling, please cheer up. It's Christmas and there's so much to look forward to . . ."

"I'm cheerful, Molly . . . really. Listen, I've got a good grip on myself now . . . literally . . ."

Her laughter is a delight to hear. I know I love her when she laughs like this.

"You're an awful man. . . . Now you make yourself a big drink and go to bed. I'll see you here tomorrow about nine."

"Right."

"Good-night, darling, and Merry Christmas."

"Merry Christmas, Molly-o!"

The bishop has removed the mitre and stepped up into the pulpit to deliver the homily. Under the lights his grey crew-cut bristles fiercely. He bites the words with his strong jaws, the muscles in his cheeks working like the gears of some perfect machine. His teeth are even and white and doubtless cavity-free. It is possible to see in him a man who believes in using dental floss after every meal.

His message is upbeat and delivered in a cranky incriminatory voice full of admonition and remand: a football coach's half-time spiel. You can tell, looking at the man, that he has no time for the thundering ironies. It develops that he is tired of the world's pessimism and despair. It is time to lift up our hearts and reawaken hope in the human breast. He puts forward his case in a tough know-it-all Navy chaplain way. I fidget as I usually do during such messages, not knowing quite how to take them. It is all very well to use a fine-sounding phrase like reawaken hope in the human breast, but what exactly does he mean, I wonder. If he were to say something like: let us each endeavour to stay awake tomorrow and put one foot in front of the other carefully so as not miss a step and fall completely on our faces, I think I would know what he means and even offer applause from my small corner. I am forced to turn the bishop off.

On the balcony the damp cold seeps up through the cement and into the soles of my Sisman loafers. At this hour the Shopping Plaza has a bereaved look about it. An abeyant melancholy seems to cling to the storefronts and to the Christmas lights which blink solemnly out at the empty parking lot. On the top of the Arcade Department Store Santa still rides his ghostly sleigh. Behind me the cooling tubes of my television set crackle faintly in the darkness.

Overhead the sky is flooded with stars. On such a night as this I used to position my telescope just so, aiming it at Ursa Major and extending an imaginary line through the two end stars of the Dipper. This way I could get a fix on the North Star, that ancient guiding light of other lonely mariners who have passed this way. Perhaps in the new year on another fine night I will take out the telescope and have another look. Right now it is enough to gaze upward and bear witness to all this light, travelling from its fiery origins with a perfect indifference, across the immensities of space and time, to strike the retinas of my eyes at this moment—to bear witness to this remarkable light and wait for sleep and try to remember what it is I was supposed to do.